===== What Happened to My Sister . . . ?

I squinted up at the blue sky. Marshmallow clouds floated lazily above, and in the distance there was the ricocheting sound of a hammer—metal against stone. Descending the stone steps, I surveyed the courtyard that I had barely seen yesterday. Within the daunting stone walls were patches of brittle, dead grass surrounded by scrubby flower beds. Though winter's visage still covered the land, there was promise that this was a more gentle place in summer.

I faced east and headed under the main gate, toward the Roman ruins in the outerworks. Surely this was where Catherine had been. Would there be any trace of her presence?

A shadow fell across my path. . . .

"IMAGINATIVE AND SURPRISING. READERS LOOKING FOR A CLASSIC GOTHIC WILL REVEL IN THIS BOOK."—Kristi Lyn Glass, *Gothic Journal*

"JERI SMITH'S BEST YET . . . A HAUNTING AND CLEVER GOTHIC."
—Kathe Robin, *Romantic Times*

Diamond Books by Jeri Smith

THE LEGACY OF HUNTER HOUSE
WITCH TREE INN
THE HAUNTING OF VICTORIA

THE HAUNTING OF VICTORIA

JERI SMITH

D
DIAMOND BOOKS, NEW YORK

If you purchased this book without a cover you should be aware that this book is stolen property. It was reported as "unsold and destroyed" to the publisher and neither the author nor the publisher has received any payment for this "stripped book."

This book is a Diamond original edition, and has never been previously published.

THE HAUNTING OF VICTORIA

A Diamond Book / published by arrangement with the author

PRINTING HISTORY
Diamond edition / March 1993

All rights reserved.
Copyright © 1993 by Jeri Smith.
This book may not be reproduced in whole or in part, by mimeograph or any other means, without permission. For information address:
The Berkley Publishing Group,
200 Madison Avenue, New York, New York 10016.

ISBN: 1-55773-871-8

Diamond Books are published by The Berkley Publishing Group, 200 Madison Avenue, New York, New York 10016. The name "DIAMOND" and its logo are trademarks belonging to Charter Communications, Inc.

PRINTED IN THE UNITED STATES OF AMERICA

10 9 8 7 6 5 4 3 2 1

Chapter One

MY SISTER, CATHERINE, was missing. It seems strange that a grown woman could inexplicably vanish, but astonishingly it did happen.

She was a medieval historian, hired by a Lord Rothesay to help him restore his old castle in England. It was rumored to be a ponderous stone fortress dating back centuries, situated on a lonely strip of land along the Kent coast. Just the thought of such an outpost conjured up images of skulduggery, tales of pirating, and visions of knights and maidens. Given her love of history, I didn't blame Catherine for accepting the post. But now she was gone, and there was no accounting for her.

There was the usual investigation and theories about her possible whereabouts—perhaps she had discovered some secret treasure buried in the castle and then left the country, maybe she—but she never turned up. There was even a short article in the London *Times* of October 31, 1888, the headline of which read: AMERICAN WOMAN MYSTERIOUSLY VANISHES AT TAVISTOCK CASTLE.

The article proclaimed that James Rothesay, Third Marquess of Wessex, and scion of Sir Walter Rothesay, chief secretary to King Henry VIII, had reported a young historian missing.

It went on to state that Catherine Ryce, newly hired at Tavistock Castle, was last glimpsed prior to the All Hallows' Eve celebration. Apparently that festivity, coming at the end of the autumn harvest, brought the entire town of Dover to the Rothesays' estate for merrymaking.

"Some cutthroat villain probably saw her and attempted to compromise her!" Father fumed after reading the article. "Then when she put up a fight . . . well, the damned fool got mad and . . . did something to her! The family's trying to protect one of the local rogues by implying that she ran away. But you and I know she didn't. I'll be damned if I believe that story! It's not like Catherine to do something so headstrong."

I could hardly determine what Catherine might have done that night, for to be honest I didn't know her well. Though Catherine was two years my senior, we were separated when I was still an infant. It's hard to fathom just what went on in those days, but it seems that Mother nearly lost her life during Catherine's birth and was warned not to have another child. Heedless of the doctor's admonishments, Mother brought me into the world. Evidently the doctor had been right because Mother passed away soon after my birth. I've been told since that Father plummeted into such depths of sorrow that he was virtually useless for quite a while. The task of our immediate care was given to our aunt and uncle in Minnesota. Catherine and I were whisked off to the Middle West for a year, at the end of which time Father came 'round and claimed me. He was torn apart at leaving Catherine behind, but she had grown so attached to her new parents, and they to her, that it would have been cruel to take her away.

"Besides," Father would say to me later, "it's still family. It's not as though I put her up for adoption."

Unfortunately Father and I lived in New York, and our visits to see Catherine were far too infrequent. We saw each other only once a year, and I grew up feeling as though she were merely a distant cousin. Though we were sisters, our interests were vastly different. She loved books and perused dry tomes of English history as eagerly as I painted watercolors.

The spindly biological thread that linked us seemed to be our only connection. Yet though I grew up with the misapplied tag of "only child" and led a lonely childhood, I was filled with remorse at the thought of losing my only

The Haunting of Victoria

sister. No more so than Father, however, who schemed and planned to solve the mystery surrounding Catherine's disappearance.

Finally he wrote directly to the marquess himself. Father explained that he was a highly esteemed artist living in New York City and that he would be honored to receive a painting commission from the Rothesay family. It wasn't difficult for him to omit that he was Catherine's father, especially since their last names were different.

Father got his answer, but it was not quite what he had in mind. The marquess was not in the market for a painting, though he was honored that a man of Father's reputation was offering his services. Instead he needed an art instructor for his niece. Could Edmund Durnham come to Tavistock Castle, work on a trial basis with his niece, Victoria, and if a satisfactory arrangement could be made, stay indefinitely?

No explanations of how old the girl was. No mention of salary. No mention of lodging arrangements.

I couldn't reason with Father about what he was resolved to do, but a vision of disaster clouded my mind. It was hardly a surprise to me when Father accepted the position. He was desperate to learn the truth about Catherine.

A week later Father stood in the entrance hall and called to me. "Anne, my dear, I'm leaving! Come and kiss me good-bye."

The afternoon sun beamed through the stained glass of our front door, splashing a rainbow of color onto my father's topper, his frock coat thrown carelessly over his arm, the valises and trunks strewn upon the floor. He turned around absentmindedly to look for his cane, which he constantly misplaced.

He looked like a friendly old wizard with his creased, kind face, steel spectacles, and trim snowy beard. He wore his Sunday best and looked the businessman he was not. I placed a hand on the banister and glimpsed him from the top of the stairs.

"Right behind you." I laughed. "Your cane is leaning against the wall, Father."

He smiled and shook his head distractedly. "Oh, yes, oh, dear, my old wits are abandoning me, I daresay!"

"You've got a lot on your mind," I said, feeling a pang of regret. Should I accompany him? I was his assistant, after all, and trouble surely lay ahead.

As I descended the stairs Father clutched his stomach and doubled over in a spasm of pain. I couldn't seem to reach him soon enough, and in that suspended moment when he hit the floor all my false notions of security came crashing down with him. When I reached him, he was unconscious.

For a week Father lay in a somnolent state, and there was no guarantee that he would live. However, I was optimistic. I telegraphed the Marquess informing him that Father was unexpectantly delayed—no mention of his illness—and I rescheduled Father's voyage in a month's time, believing that he would be well by then. My premature hopes were painfully dashed because at week's end Father died. The doctor's diagnosis: a heart attack.

Grief washed over me like a wave, and when it subsided a little, I realized how bitterly I would miss him and how alone in the world I would be. Managing to keep a precise, practical head about me, I arranged the burial service and sold the town house and furniture. His paintings were his only possessions of real value—and the best ones had been sold long ago. His estate left me with very little.

Still feeling stunned and uneasy, I tried to imagine how I would earn a living. Though I had worked closely with Father and under his tutorship had become an accomplished artist myself—recognized in art circles—I had never given a thought to money.

Not long after Father's death, a door opened for me. I received another letter from the marquess expressing displeasure that Father had been detained, and that he was eagerly awaiting Father on his next scheduled arrival. No delay could be permitted this time.

It was an urgent summons, and I took it as a golden opportunity, immediately deciding to go in Father's place. There was no time for fearful indecision, for writing the marquess to say that Edmund Durnham's daughter would be arriving instead. Laying aside my bombazine gown and stepping out of mourning, I prepared myself for the journey.

Three weeks after leaving New York Harbor, I found myself on the final leg of the voyage I had so urgently arranged; I'd traveled across the Atlantic aboard a steamer, arriving the night before at the port of Bristol and finding a suitable hotel. The next afternoon I'd boarded the train that would bring me to Dover—my last stop.

Now as I followed the accommodating porter through the pouring rain to the Dover station, I wondered if I had made the right decision after all. It's not too late, I thought wretchedly, I can still go back ...

"Someone'll be here to meetya, is that right?" the porter asked as he set my bags on a wooden bench inside the station.

"Yes, I'm sure a driver will be here any moment," I answered, toying with the clasp on my framed handbag.

I was exhausted and looked every bit of my twenty-five years. I had saved my most expensive traveling suit for today, having purchased a slate-gray toque to match, suede gloves trimmed in lace, and luscious satin barrette boots.

Despite all my preparations to look pretty I knew neither the worry lines nor the paleness of my skin after many sleepless nights could be erased.

As if to heighten my feeling of doom, a terrible spring storm had descended upon the train outside Folkestone. Rain poured as if from celestial buckets, pitchforks of lightning lit the sky, and thunder echoed like kettledrums. I was disappointed at not having a view of the white cliffs of Dover, but there would be other days to explore the coast. If I were asked to stay, of course ...

"Tavistock Castle, hmmm?" the porter asked cryptically.

Startled, I looked up at him. "Yes, why, is there something I should know?"

"Well, I don' mean to alarm ya' but—"

The station door banged violently open and a squat, thickset Englishman wearing a dripping oilskin hurried up to us.

Glancing suspiciously from the porter to me and back again, he queried in cockney English, "Madam? Are you . . . American?"

I stood quickly. "Yes, I am. You must be from Tavistock Castle?"

"That I am! My nime's Gavin, madam."

The porter silently bowed to me in an effort at courtesy, then moved back out into the storm. It was only a moment before the whistle sounded and the train was pulling away. What had he been about to say?

There was a pause before I said politely, "Pleased to meet you. I am Anne Durnham from New York."

The driver eyed me warily. I felt my resolve crumble.

"But I wasn't tol' to git no lidy. Master tol' me to—" He stopped and looked around the depot that smelled faintly of tobacco smoke and polish. "Is there a *Mister* Durn'am?"

I forced a tone of nonchalance and smiled. "No, there must be a misunderstanding. The marquess sent for me several months ago."

This was the first of the obstacles I would have to face. Though the Rothesays had expected a man, I was not going to disclose my deception to the driver. There was time enough to assure the master himself of my capabilities.

Pulling my silk mantle tightly around me, I said with self-control, "I have only this bag and a wooden easel. I can manage the easel if you carry my portmanteau."

There was an uneasy pause.

"Yes, of course. But I can' say 'ow 'appy Master James is goina' be about this!"

I longed to asked the driver about the marquess. It would have been helpful to know what sort of person he was, but some innate politeness held my curiosity at bay.

In anxious silence I followed the driver to the waiting trap. Its high thin wheels and large, sleek body reminded me more of an eighteenth-century coach than a modern one.

The Haunting of Victoria

The rain was not so thoroughly soaking as it had been earlier, and I was glad to be warm and dry inside the conveyance. As I settled myself in the rich leather seat my carefully checked grief over Father's death welled up in me again. Tears burned my eyes, and I dabbed my face with a handkerchief. I must be sensible and not allow my emotions to overwhelm me, I told myself.

"G'dap! A little rine ain't goina' 'urt ya'!" Gavin shouted to the matching grays as we lurched forward.

As I peered expectantly out the window I felt my anguish evaporate. There, before me, was the Kent countryside— so aptly named "the garden of England." Between silver-green poplars lining the road I could see fields of budding fruit trees, colorless in the rain. Fallow fields dotted with capped oast houses stretched to the horizon, and ruins of brick-and-timber buildings were tucked into an occasional hollow. Abruptly we turned up a narrow road and the vista opened. Falling away from the lane, a tract of rolling downs gave way to gray sky and the foamy green sea below.

Above us stood the castle. A tremor of excitement brought me to the edge of my seat. There are moments in life when fear dissolves a little and the need to confront a challenge replaces it. Momentarily I was unafraid and almost reckless. Common sense and logic were tossed aside, and I threw back my head and laughed.

"What could be so frightening?" I asked aloud as I surveyed the castle with wonder.

The image before me was that of some battlemented city in a medieval drawing. High towers, sloping roofs, and chimneys crowded above crenellated walls. Enveloped in silence, the castle wore the semblance of a dream, making me as eager as a schoolgirl to pass under those beaked turrets and explore the castle's inner sanctums.

What was I thinking? I shuddered suddenly. My sister had *disappeared* inside those stony walls!

I tried to calm my racing pulse as the buggy swayed over a medieval bridge. It lent a splendid view of ditch and bank. We passed under the gateway, and I surveyed with marvel its arched transoms, ornamental moldings, and brick casements.

We turned sharply and traveled up a lofty grade before slowing in front of the gatehouse. The latter building was connected to a dark ragstone curtain; ruins of stone galleries and parapets jutted out along the rim of the wall. Ancient military defenses, I mused. How ghastly to be a victim of boiling water or plummeting arrows! I was thrilled, yet repulsed.

We bounded into an inner cobblestone courtyard and came to a halt.

The door opened suddenly to reveal Gavin's grim face. "Looks as if the rine 'as stopped, madam."

"Oh, yes, it has!" A chill wind was beginning to break up the clouds.

I hoped he hadn't noticed the emotion in my face when he helped me down. Could Catherine be a prisoner inside these weather-darkened walls . . . locked away in a pestilent, damp dungeon? A cold gust chilled me, and I shivered. Oh, Catherine! Where are you?

"There are two main gites—the King's and the Queen's." The driver waved a hand at the walls surrounding us. "The one we come through is the King's Gite. It's the main one, of course, leadin' in from town and runnin' through Fitzwilliams, Godsfoe, and Treasurer's towers. Up ahead there is the keep, or livin' quarters, where the Rothesays reside."

It was hard to believe that anyone lived in the looming fortress before us.

"It's magnificent," I said, hardly able to breathe.

"And the gitekeeper's lodge is built right into the gite where we come in." He hoisted my bag down from the box.

Fascinated, I turned to view the gatekeeper's house at the entrance. Though elegant modern windows and a pretty little balcony made the tower more inhabitable, something evil seemed to loom there. As I scanned the facade a movement caught my eye. The nail-studded door opened slightly and a shadow materialized in the doorway. Someone was watching me! Shaken, I quickly turned away.

What could be more natural than someone peering at a new employee? It is absurd to be so frightened, I admonished myself. Unless that interest is not friendly . . . for does someone suspect me of searching for Catherine?

"And over there's the lighthouse, and the ruins next to it are part of the original castle. The master . . . he's interested in restorin' any of the castle that cin be saved." Gavin pointed. As the churlish wind blew up I could smell the sea.

"There 'ave been archaeologists and 'istorians down 'ere pokin' 'round tryin' to find somethin'. There's talk that family jewels was 'idden just before the Restoration. They're 'ere somewhere, 'idden by the original Rothesays so's the Church couldn't steal the gems durin' the Inquisition!"

"How interesting!" I exhaled, thinking of Catherine.

He peered at me closely. "Somethin' even more interestin' 'appened just recently. Oh . . . five, six months ago. One of the young women workin' 'ere disappeared one night."

I tried to keep from faltering. "Yes . . . yes, I read something about it."

"There was a great fuss. It was very upsetting, mind you. 'Appened on All 'allows' Eve. No one 'as a clue where she went."

"Is there . . . no trace of her? I mean how could she have just vanished?" I felt my face warm suddenly. How foolish to appear so intrigued! "It seems rather unusual, that's all," I said quickly.

He looked down at my bags. "Don't know, madam. Don't know. It's a mystery, it is."

"The sea smells wonderful." I decided to change the subject before I betrayed myself.

"Yes, when the wind blows this way, it's most pleasant."

He handed me my easel, and when I took it my hands were trembling.

"It'll be this way, madam."

I followed him in awe as we made for a wooden door set between twin towers. My boot heels echoed loudly against the cobblestones as a blast of wind sent dead leaves whirling against my skirts. My excitement had been crushed and dread had replaced it.

He pushed open the heavy door. "Follow me," he said.

We entered an arched anteroom where three spectacularly antlered stags' heads were displayed. Their magnificence was lost on me, as I never prized hunting.

"Oh!" I said, practically recoiling.

"Yes, them's 're beauties!" He picked up a burning taper from a teak sideboard. "Now, mind yer step as we pass the brewhouse and bakery on yer left," he said as he led me into a corridor.

The dim glow of the candle lent little light, but I could see that the rooms were hung with worn tapestries and more sets of antlers. Deep, arched recesses were cut into the walls. Ovens, I thought, shuddering with pleasure at the bewitching castle.

There were only two narrow window embrasures in the corridor, and deep shadows engulfed us as we ascended well-worn steps to an upper level.

"If you'll look up, madam, you'll see holes cut in the rooftop." He held the light higher, and I glanced at the lofty ceiling. "Murder holes, they call 'em. If you was an enemy of the family that lived 'ere, and you got through the outer gate and into this entranceway, you'd most likely be trapped 'ere. Then you'd either be shot with an arrow or burned to death with boiling pitch!" He laughed.

I smiled stiffly. Oh, Catherine! What have they done with you?

At the top of the stairs we moved down a short passage hung with green velveteen draperies. He pulled them open to reveal a door.

"If you will wait ere . . ." And he disappeared.

I was alone. He had set the candle at my feet, but beyond its circle of lemony light the gloom seemed to stretch forever. I didn't dare look back into the darkness. Suddenly a draft caught the flame and made it dance about, almost extinguishing it.

"Oh," I whispered. "Don't go out!" Were there ghosts

The Haunting of Victoria

at Tavistock Castle? It certainly seemed a likely place for them. "Perhaps there are," I said aloud, tentatively. "But they can't harm me . . ."

A flood of warm light fell upon me as Gavin opened the door again and signaled for me to enter. He plucked the candle from the dim corridor as I gladly moved away from the shadows and into an enormous medieval hall.

There was a magnificent beamed ceiling that rose at least three stories above us; weapons hung on one limewashed wall, while an exuberantly decorated oak screen covered another. Deeply worn wooden posts for torches stood at regular intervals about the room, and glittering chandeliers hung from the rafters. The tiled floor was laid with brilliant rugs and in the center was a rustic octagonal hearth surrounded by a stone curb. On another wall was a working fireplace in which a snapping fire leaped and hissed.

A broad staircase wound down from an upper level, and a polished suit of armor graced the landing.

" . . . someone'll be with you in a moment," Gavin was saying. "I'll git yer bags t' yer room by the time you've 'ad tea."

He left me again. I was more than a little afraid. I had rehearsed my speeches and explanations, but now I must face the Marquess of Wessex. He would be, no doubt, a man who felt comfortable in this haunted atmosphere. A formidable man, someone who would not like surprises.

"I must remain calm," I exhaled raggedly. My future—and most likely Catherine's—hung on my conduct in the next few minutes. I went to the fireplace and pulled off my gloves.

I am able to live without a man's approval, I thought with resolve. There is no reason to fall to pieces when I meet the marquess. For hadn't I learned, two years ago when my beau, Thomas, died, that there are other things in life besides dedicating oneself to a man? Perhaps if Thomas had lived, I would have become an ordinary housewife—content to put aside my dreams for him. How foolish to think that I would have been happy living so! But things change, and now I would have to prove myself after all.

Footsteps. I would have to turn around soon. Dignity—retain my dignity and don't appear too eager, I told myself nervously. My glance touched the colossal overmantel, the gilt clock flanked by carved lovers, the twin leaded windows far above me, but I could not give these treasures my full attention. I twisted my hands before the flames and felt them warm slightly.

Again there was silence, though I knew someone now stood directly behind me. "There has been a misunderstanding." It was a mellifluous female voice.

I flew around in startled surprise, and my eyes lit on a stunning woman. Her regal appearance made me catch my breath, for her canary-yellow evening gown enhanced the color of her thick red hair, porcelain skin, and the amber flecks in her eyes. Tiny diamonds sparkled at her earlobes and around her neck.

"We were expecting *Mister* Durnham, the renowned artist."

I clutched my sodden gloves for support. "I'm afraid that is quite impossible."

"I see. Perhaps you will be good enough to explain?"

"Mr. Durnham is my father, and he died two months ago. I am here to assume his position as teacher. I have a university education and have been trained by Father, so you see I am very qualified."

She looked alarmed. "My deepest condolences, Miss Durnham. I hope I do not insult you by speaking plainly, but we were counting on an expert to teach Victoria. Someone who truly has skill as a painter. She is not untalented and wants to learn. She only needs someone with talent to guide her."

She smiled suddenly and a vision of warmth and radiance emerged, as if another being dwelled inside her.

"I see your position, of course," I replied, trying to quell my uneasiness. "I have brought the necessary references and testimonials. Also some watercolors and oils for your inspection. I would hate to be turned away before having

The Haunting of Victoria

had a chance to meet your niece. I tend to work rather well with children."

Suddenly the great oaken door opened, and as we both glanced up simultaneously the figure of a man emerged. He was a tall man in trousers and pea coat, drenched to the skin. His leather boots were caked with mud and a film of chalky soot covered him. I assumed he was the stable master, yet he exuded such careless impertinence, such easy grace, that I couldn't be sure.

Impatiently brushing a tendril of black hair from his forehead, he flashed a smile at the woman and held out a gloved hand. In his palm some tiny object caught the light and shone.

As she exclaimed in sheer delight and moved quickly to him, he coolly looked at me for the first time.

All his being seemed to be focused in his dark, snapping eyes, and his masculine face was unyielding, void of expression—or of warmth. As he watched me from over her bent head neither of us made the polite move to introduce ourselves.

A rush of color rose in my cheeks, but I held his look stubbornly and told myself to stop trembling like a fool. He could win any woman over with those eyes, I told myself. Yet he was undoubtedly a roguish character, someone to be ignored at all cost.

I held my head high in an effort to compose myself before the master of the castle—the marquess himself—entered.

"I don't believe we've met," he finally said with a hint of smile.

"Good day," I said, inclining my head, offering nothing more. Maybe arrogance would hide my anxiety.

"You must be a friend of Margaret's? I am James Rothesay. Please," he continued, not unkindly, after a pause. "Have a chair. You look as if you've seen a ghost."

Chapter Two

So THIS WAS the famous Englishman! I tried to turn away, but his raw vitality and unassuming charm made me watch him against my wishes.

He pulled out a magnificent oak-framed armchair that must have seen generations of kings and offered it to me.

"Thank you." I exhaled and sat, watching the marquess as he removed his drenched coat, tossing it over a pair of matching red velvet chairs against the wall.

With my heart slamming against my rib cage, my courage failing fast, I tried to speak. "You see—"

Margaret whirled around abruptly, her eyes shining like stars. "Please excuse my lack of introductions! I am Margaret Rothesay," she said to me, and added, "James, this is Miss Durnham, daughter of Edward, the ... you know, Edward Durnham, the artist."

The gentleness disappeared from his face and a stern, hard-edged look replaced it. He was the king now. He might have been looking at me from a long-dim past as we stood in a hall of mirrors.

His dark brow was furrowed; his face was blank, impossible to read. Finally he gave a quick, mirthless laugh and said tonelessly, "I see."

"My father ..." I stopped to clear my throat. His coolness made me lose my poise, but I was resolved that he would never know it. "My father lost his life very suddenly, and I have come in his stead."

He crossed his arms over his chest and frowned. "You would have saved us a great deal of trouble and embarrassment by writing us of your arrival."

The dreaded moment had come. I was being dismissed. I stood suddenly, feeling that I must have more equal footing to state my case.

"As I have mentioned to Lady Rothesay, I am very qualified—having studied with my father, and having earned acclaim in the art world for several of my paintings."

"I've no doubt that you are very talented," he said flatly. "Oh, you've dropped your glove."

As he reached to pick it up, and I leaned out to retrieve it from him, the satin strap on my corset slipped down, and I could feel it sagging under my dress. I blushed suddenly at feeling so vulnerable, so out of control.

"Thank you," I said when he gave me the damp glove. "I suppose England is not so modern as America, for in my country women are free to work at many jobs. No one thought less of me because I was an artist and helped my father in his painting commissions."

My armor was up. How I disliked challenging a man of his position, but my entire livelihood was at stake.

His eyes flashed. "You presume a lot, Miss Durnham. But I am not surprised. American women seem to be rather forthright in their actions—as though afraid their independence is threatened."

I felt a tingling down my spine. He obviously enjoyed seeing me beg for a position that I did not want. All I desired was to find Catherine, procure enough money for steamboat passage, and get out of here. Damn this stubborn man who was making my life so difficult!

I bit my lip and said, "Perhaps you're right, but my work is very good, and after traveling for three weeks, I hardly feel it is fair to turn me away—when you have discovered I am not a man."

No one said a word. My tone was too venomous, perhaps, my look at the marquess too defiant.

I had to back down, and trying to soften my tone, I said, "Painting is thrilling work to me. I think anyone who becomes as absorbed in their work as I will naturally make a good teacher. I would like a trial period at least."

"Darling, I agree!" Lady Rothesay approached the marquess—I assumed he was her husband—and hung lovingly on his arm. "I'm sure she is perfectly capable of teaching Victoria. The least we can do is to let her try."

Her purring voice, her doelike eyes upturned to him, her sympathetic smile made me forget that only moments ago she, too, was ready to let me go.

His lips twisted into a smile as he looked down at her. To my surprise, there were dimples cut into his craggy face. "You are both wrong. I have not said no. I have said only—"

"That Miss Durnham's coming here was a mistake," Margaret finished.

"That is not what I said." Though his boyish charm had returned, there was an unforgiving note in his voice. "I have not said I would not employ a woman! Or that Miss Durnham should leave. That was your suggestion." He looked at me.

"I must be honest. I was counting on Edward Durnham since he is so renowned in his profession. Did you know, Miss Durnham, that I own one of his paintings? Just purchased a fortnight ago at an auction house in London? It is a sketch of a young girl with long, disheveled hair and eyes brimming with tears. It is quite beautiful."

I felt as though the wind had been knocked out of me. That was one of several versions of a childhood portrait Father had painted of me. He had sold them all, many years ago, to a wealthy count who had been an avid collector of modern art.

"No, I was unaware you owned something... of Father's," I said, still breathless.

"I will take you to see it and all the other paintings in our picture gallery," he stated.

"I would like that," I replied, fumbling with my gloves. The Rothesays watched me in silence.

Finally the marquess looked at his wife, then queried me in a gentler voice, "Knowing that your father is unable to come, I must ask, Miss Durnham, if you have any experience as a teacher? With children who are quite capable, but are not working up to their capacities?"

"I would call Victoria a young woman rather than a child, wouldn't you, dear?" Margaret dazzled a smile at Rothesay.

Slanting a look down at her, he said, "Perhaps." To me, he tossed, "She has just turned eleven, you know, Miss Durnham. An independent sort of girl at her age."

A young, strong-willed girl, probably terribly spoiled, terribly pretty, and extremely fond of herself, I thought miserably. It hardly seemed like an attractive job. But mine was not an attractive situation. I was penniless, alone. I couldn't afford to be turned away. I couldn't even afford the passage back to America. And I had to find Catherine. . . .

"It sounds like a very stimulating situation. I'm sure Victoria and I will get along very well."

"You haven't answered my question, Miss Durnham."

I gazed levelly at Rothesay. "Which is?"

"Have you experience as a teacher?"

"Lord Rothesay, I will be honest. I have no experience teaching children, nor had my father. I enjoy children and have always found them to be particularly easy to be around. Since I am a woman, it will be easier for me to communicate with her than it would have been for my father. As for my skills as an artist—" Margaret and Rothesay exhanged heated looks, and I lowered my glance. "I have been told that I am quite accomplished."

There was a hissing sound as a log slipped in the grate.

"And confident." His voice had a glimmer of amusement in it.

"If that is a compliment, thank you. If it was meant as an insult, then it is not the worst I could receive."

"I assure you that my comment was meant as a compliment. And, please, Miss Durnham, do not look at me so sternly. I find self-assurance admirable in a woman."

Suddenly I was ashamed of my defensive posture. The man who had seemed so intimidating when he first appeared now seemed kind and even reassuring—as if he had warmed toward me. Had he changed his opinion so fast?

"Thank you," I said quietly, feeling my cheeks warm.

"Oh, do stay, Miss Durnham. We want you to stay!" Lady Rothesay sounded on edge; her voice was high, like a stretched-out string. For a stinging moment I wondered if she was afraid of the marquess.

"Perhaps, James, we could set her up for a month? If Victoria shows improvement during that time . . ." Margaret looked eagerly at Rothesay and back to me.

She was having a hard time getting his attention for his eyes were fastened on me. I wanted to look away, but felt that I might lose the challenge—or whatever his goading look was calculated to mean.

"Miss Durnham." He left Margaret's side, and I saw her small movement of disappointment. With deliberation, he walked toward me.

It was an effort not to step back as he approached. My feet were planted firmly, and the floor seemed to burn under them. I had learned long ago that the way to get a man's attention was not to defer to him.

He stopped at the fireplace—very close to me—and placed his hand on the stone overmantel. With his forefinger he slowly traced the carved dancing nymphs. When he spoke, his voice was gravelly.

"We have not been fair with you," he said to the dying fire.

I looked at Margaret, who cocked her lovely head in question. Her eyes moved between the two of us.

"Victoria has had a recent—"

"She has been very ill," Margaret said in a thin voice.

Rothesay narrowed his eyes and lowered his head. For a fleeting second I thought he trembled. Almost before I registered what had seemed like anguish settle on his countenance, his face cleared. He turned to Margaret with a correct, perfunctory smile.

"We believe that Victoria suffered a great shock on All Hallows' Eve. Since the day following that celebration she has been very unlike herself. Before that she was a bright, effervescent child."

The Haunting of Victoria

I tried to subdue the nervousness I felt at the mention of All Hallows' Eve.

"We—Margaret and I—wanted to hire your father because Victoria always loved art, and we thought he could rekindle her interest in painting. Victoria is my niece, Margaret and my deceased brother's daughter. I love her as my own, of course, and that's why I am so concerned. Only recently has she become unbalanced, extremely difficult, responding to no one. Her tutor and governess can do nothing for her. We are desperate. We thought your father could inspire her to paint again—and to come alive again."

He crossed his arms over his chest, his stare remaining fixed on some distant point above Margaret's head.

Though I knew now where the marquess's anguish came from, I was surprised to learn that Margaret was Victoria's mother, and not her aunt, as I had assumed. I had undoubtedly misconstrued Margaret's position in thinking she was the marquess's wife. A darting recollection of the marquess's letter to my father strengthened my conclusion. *He* would like a teacher for his niece, *he* would be grateful for his arrival as soon as possible. No mention of his wife.

The marquess was speaking again. "From Victoria's earliest years she has wandered out upon the grassy downs, paper and easel in hand, and painted for hours. She is quite talented, but for many months she has not even touched a canvas or paintbrush. Nor has she done much else. Except sleep too little and eat even less. It's been six months."

"Six months too long," Margaret said, moving toward us tentatively.

"Last winter when we received a letter from your father querying us about a commission to paint a portrait, I could hardly believe our luck! Here was Edward Durnham—famous American artist—looking for work. I decided to hire him immediately as a teacher. I purposely left out mention of salary. I was—and still am—prepared to pay well." He turned a sober face to me. "I only want to see my niece happy again."

"Oh, yes, that is most important." Margaret stood in front of us, her hands clasped tightly together.

"I am sorry to hear of your niece's poor health," I said quietly.

"Perhaps now that you can see the . . . urgency of our situation, you can better understand why I was surprised and, at first, angered by your deception. Though I am sure now, even though I am not familiar with your work, that you will do well with Victoria."

It was hard-earned praise, and with self-possession I faced them. "Lord Rothesay, I did what any honest woman would do. I worked so closely with Father that I practically became an extension of him. When he died, my duty was to fulfill his obligations. This was one of them. I am not the sort of person who deceives."

I thought I saw a flicker of surprise cross his face, but it dissolved when Margaret spoke.

"Miss Durnham, no offense was meant," she said. "If it is agreed, James"—Margaret turned to Rothesay—"she will stay for . . . let's say a month?"

Rothesay nodded, regarding me. Once again I met his cool appraisal without wavering.

"Would you consider devoting yourself to Victoria for a month? If she shows improvement in her painting—as well as her disposition—you will be asked to stay."

He offered a monthly salary that caused me to gasp involuntarily. It was more generous than I had hoped—even from a man as rich as the marquess. For a few seconds I was pleased, delighted even. A month would be enough time to find Catherine and travel home to safety.

"You are very generous," I said to him. "Thank you, I will be pleased to accept this, ah, situation."

The marquess hesitated a moment, watching me still, then, in a fluid movement he walked to the door and yanked the braided bell pull that hung there. "Eva will take you up, and we'll have tea sent to you immediately. I wonder . . ." A hint of smile crossed his face. "Would you be willing to meet Victoria right away? After you've had some refreshment?"

"Of course," I answered as we were interrupted by a round, earnest servant woman who came bounding into the room.

Huffing, she turned her intelligent face to me, surveying me politely while her master instructed her to lead me to my rooms. She was introduced as the head housemaid. She bobbed a courteous head toward me, and I nodded in return. Under Eva's close scrutiny I felt mildly comforted. There was a keen light in her chocolate-brown eyes, and worldly wisdom suffused her aging face.

"There is a custom in England to shake hands when an agreement is made." Rothesay turned to me with his hand outstretched.

Careful not to show my surprise, I clasped his powerful hand in mine and felt a rush of warmth burn up my arm.

I mumbled an inane comment about how we in America shake hands also, to seal a business proposition. Whatever spell had been cast upon me was quickly broken as our hands dropped, and the marquess spoke again—almost brusquely.

"It is better if we do not go with you to meet Victoria. I think it will be easier for you to get acquainted."

"A marvelous suggestion, James." Margaret had reassumed her position next to the marquess and a victorious smile lit her face. "Please, join us for dinner, won't you? We don't have any engagements this evening, and we would like to get to know you better."

It was agreed that I would dine with them, the time and place arranged, and I was at once following Eva up the great staircase. With every step I took, I could feel their eyes upon me, but I didn't dare look back.

As Eva led the way up the stairs I laid my hand on the carved banister. The maid smiled reassuringly at me, and I continued to follow her.

At the top of the staircase, a marble hall rose to the full height of the castle keep. Oil paintings, with beautifully embellished wooden frames, lined the walls, and I stopped a moment to examine them closer. One particularly stood out to my eyes. It was a vibrant medieval scene of a gathering of peasants dancing in a barn. I gasped when I saw the famous scrawled signature.

"Brueghel," I said out loud.

"You must see the picture gallery, madam," Eva suggested. "There are paintings by many esteemed artists. Rembrandt, Titian, Jan Steen, Rubens. You should ask the master to show you."

"He has already offered. I've always marveled at the Dutch painters and have even tried to emulate them. I studied the classical school of painting."

"No doubt you are talented as an artist, or the master would not have hired one so young."

I blushed at her words, but skepticism made me wonder if she were only trying to discover my age. I was not about to disclose that I was twenty-five years old and had never been married.

Eva led me through a narrow, dark passage to an ancient stone stairway that wound like a coil toward the top of a tower. Feeling a sudden dampness in my bones, I glanced up at the worn stone steps. There was a deep, narrow window embrasure that lent indirect gray light.

"Be careful, madam. The stairs are steep and uneven."

Cautiously I touched the cold walls for support as I climbed. "This seems to be part of the original castle," I said, trying to appear nonchalant.

Eva stopped suddenly and turned to me. "Actually the original castle was a fortress built by the Romans. Later it was rebuilt by William of Normandy. Only recently have the ruins of William's fortifications been found—over on the south side of the lighthouse. Relics have been dug up, too: a pottery piece, a metal belt buckle, a gold ring. All this has been discovered just since Miss Ryce—the lady historian—came. It's strange, though, right after she determined the date of the medieval castle, rebuilt by William, she disappeared, and no one else has been able to find much since."

She paused a moment, shivering.

My heart plummeted. *Miss Ryce—the lady historian?*

The Haunting of Victoria 23

As if she heard my thoughts, Eva said hollowly, "The woman was here only briefly. American girl. She was most unladylike. Always digging and climbing about like one of the men. Very forward in her manner. Can't help thinking someone got tired of her prying and meddling and, well... who knows? It does seem strange that she just up and vanished—like that." Snapping her fingers, she glanced at me. "Madam, don't worry. I know all American women are not like her. You have no need to look so concerned."

"Don't I?"

"Let me take you to your rooms."

Abruptly she turned away from me, and we came to the top of the stairs. In silence we moved down a short arched passage, our footfalls echoing on the stone floor. At the end of the corridor she paused and threw open a heavy door.

"This is the room reserved for guests."

I exhaled raggedly at the sight of my quarters. A golden carved four-poster bed stood regally in the room's center, its shimmering drapes tied back. Faded woven rugs were thrown over the tiled floors, and the timbered ceiling was painted with the rich blues and yellows of the Rothesay coat of arms. Though the windows were large, little light seeped through, for the upper parts were leaded glass, the lower fitted with wooden shutters. Several gas lamps were placed on gleaming tables about the room, and a new fire burned in the stone grate. My portmanteau and easel stood next to a walnut wardrobe.

"A room fit for a king!" I said in awe.

"Madam, it is one of the few rooms in the West Range that has been restored completely. Supposedly, it was once used for visiting lords. A bit intimidating, isn't it?" she asked, going to a paneled wall. "The water closet is here." She pulled open a door set inconspicuously in the wood.

I smiled in relief at the modern plumbing and the oversized tub.

"Over here"—she pointed to a tiny recess in the opposite wall—"was the oratory, where visiting lords would pray before sleeping, and the door next to it, right here—" She pulled open a narrow door with a tug. "It sticks sometimes—is a secret passageway."

A current of musky air hit me, and I recoiled in shock. A dark hole gaped at us, and fear, like a hand around my neck, threatened to choke me.

I did not try to disguise the anxiety I felt for my missing sister, nor did I give any thought to the pinched strain in my voice when I spoke. "This passageway... have the historians seen it? I mean, it seems a likely place to search for clues to the castle's history?"

She grabbed a candle off a table and lit it with a taper. "One would think so, but no, very few people have seen this passageway or know that it exists. And it's not my place to tell them. I just didn't want you to open the wrong door and injure yourself. Follow me."

I stepped out into the gloom, the halo of light illuminating the murk. We stood on a stone landing, and I could see by her flickering candle that a winding staircase, narrower and rougher than the one we had just climbed, rose up into darkness one way and plummeted back down toward more darkness.

"At the top of these stairs is Victoria's chamber. Of course, there is another, more pleasant entrance to her rooms. If you take the stairs down, you'll come to the ancient cross-house guardroom, which leads to an outside door. This secret passageway would have been the visiting lord's private entranceway to the garden below—or to his lady's bedchamber above."

"It's a menacing atmosphere, isn't it?" I shuddered. "As though an apparition of a medieval king will materialize any moment."

"Yes, it does seem so. And so easy to think that in a house as old as this one."

She hurried me inside, closing the door once more and setting down the candle.

At her request I handed her my damp coat, gloves shoved in the pockets, and watched in silence as she hung it by the fire. Filled with dark dread, I was about to ask if Catherine had slept here, but Eva spoke again.

"Madam, do you believe in ghosts?" she asked suddenly.

"I cannot deny that in a place such as this—"

"Yes. A place such as this," she answered cryptically. "I am a cynical woman, madam. I have lived too long not to be, but there are rumors that the ghost of a sixteenth-century priest roams the castle at night. There is whispered gossip about how this, er, phantom wears a hooded robe worn by executioners during the Inquisition, and that he is searching for his lady love."

A flicker of superstitious fear lit her eyes, and I looked away nervously. Why was she telling me this?

"Do you believe the rumors?" I asked, meeting her look again.

"I don't know. But, to speak frankly, there was the disappearance of the girl, Miss Ryce, you know, the historian, and with these stories of..."

"Yes?" I pressed her.

"I just wonder if Miss Ryce—"

A sharp rap at the door shook me out of my skin. Eva's purposeful voice rang out—"Enter"—and the door opened to reveal a tall, sallow-skinned undermaid with a tray.

"Aw!" She bowed slightly, then carried the tray to a side table by the bed. "Please forgive me, Missus Eva. I didn' know you was 'ere. Madam," she said to me, "I've brought tea."

"Thank you, Jobelle. I was just leaving Miss Durnham." Eva moved toward the door with the maid, Jobelle, at her heels. "If there is anything you need, madam, please call me," Eva said.

"Oh, Eva, there is one thing." A sense of foreboding made me tremble, but I had to be direct. "Did the American girl stay here... in this room?"

There was a moment of dead silence as Eva grappled with her thoughts. "No, the historians are lodged in the weaver's cottage at the edge of the south wall. Like all the others, she saw this room only once."

Was my interest in Catherine showing? "I see."

"I will leave you now. The bell is next to your bed if you need me. I hope you enjoy your stay." And with a stiff smile Eva was gone.

Quickly I fumbled with the sagging satin strap under my dress, and when it was put back into place, I went to the windows.

"Catherine!" I whispered. In the thick light of dusk I made out a jagged wall in the distance and a sloping hillside beyond. I opened the bottom shutter to feel the cold, clean air on my face. A month was an eternity. But I would find Catherine in that time, and then we could leave together.

Chapter Three

▅▅▅▅ IT DIDN'T TAKE long to fortify myself on the English tea and biscuits, after which I bathed, pulled my hair up to a tidy knot, and dressed in a plain écru gown. Though the gown was hopelessly plain, it was trimmed with ribbons of lace and sported a fairly stiff bustle. It was the best I could hope for in evening dress. I was unsure whether I would be summoned to meet Victoria first or be called to dinner with the Rothesays. Either way I could not sit calmly.

Deciding to make use of my restless energy, I unfolded the little wooden easel Father had so lovingly built for me and unpacked the rolls of canvas. Hoping the gods would forgive me, I set up my makeshift studio in the arched alcove, where the visiting lords had once prayed. I had brought with me all the little bottles of paint powder I owned, and as I lined them carefully on the floor I reminded myself to ask for an oilcloth to cover the tiles.

I pulled out from my trunk the flat portfolio thick with watercolors and oils. It contained my favorite paintings. I decided that I would show off my inspired collection and set a few of them up against the paneled walls. Then I lit the candle in the wall sconce, and when I stepped back to survey my work space, I was filled with a feeling of happy anticipation.

How difficult could my stay be? I wondered, clasping my hands together.

My awaited summons came, and I grabbed my portfolio. Eva led me once again to another unexplored realm of the castle. Down the shadowy ancient corridor, up more winding stairs, and into another suite of magnificent rooms.

Though Victoria's bedchamber resembled mine, it was, without a doubt, a girl's room. My quick perusal took in billowing lace curtains, blue-and-cream bubble lamps, a four-poster covered with a cheerful counterpane, leather books lining one wall, sad-faced teddy bears stuffed into the shelved alcove, a lovely wooden dollhouse, and most splendid of all, a red velvet dolls' perambulator carrying three pouting dolls dressed in brilliant brocade.

Eva shot me a frustrated glance. Victoria was nowhere to be seen. "Her illness has made her flighty, I am sorry to say. Heaven knows where she's hiding." She began to search the sitting room.

My eyes lit on the closed bathroom door. To my surprise it opened slowly and the nimble figure of a young woman stepped out awkwardly. Dressed in a frivolous gown of white ruffles, auburn hair floating about her shoulders, she stared at me with such bewildered intensity that I was struck with a sort of terror.

Reluctant and yet drawn to her, I moved toward her. "Hello, I am Miss Durnham. Your new art teacher."

My voice trilled through the room like the unwelcome blast of a steam engine, and she merely watched me, her dark, deep-set eyes full of suspicion.

"Oh, there you are!" Eva bounded into the room and signaled to the girl to sit down.

The girl broke eye contact with me and, without a flicker of expression, obeyed Eva's wave of her arm. She sat in a tufted armchair close to her bed.

I was uncomfortable. The girl seemed mysteriously remote: her movements were slow and trancelike as though she suffered a sort of mental illness. She had the look about her of someone who did not fit into the conventional groove. Everything I observed increased my discomfort and made me want to flee.

"Here, madam, sit on the bed, there. Yes, that's fine."

Obeying Eva's instructions, I sat on the bed, facing the strange girl. I laid my portfolio next to me, and she fastened her avid gaze on me again. I smiled awkwardly in response.

The Haunting of Victoria

"A very pretty room you have here," I said.

Eva had bustled over to Victoria's play area and returned with a thick tablet and a crayon.

Miss Durnham is your new art teacher. She has come from America to teach you. You must make her feel welcome in her new home, Eva scrawled across the page.

Victoria snatched the pad from Eva and read it with a keen interest. I sent a puzzled glance to Eva, which she answered with a sad smile.

"Victoria is deaf and dumb. But it is only a recent development. She is also plagued by frequent nightmares and an unnatural restlessness, too. No one can understand why she suffers so or from where her condition originates. Perhaps it is simply a hereditary weakness of the brain."

"Has she been seen by doctors?" I asked.

"Oh, yes. Several physicians have seen her recently. But there has been no conclusion as to her illness. Meanwhile her last governess left in a frustrated fury, and I have been left to look after her needs in addition to my regular staff duties. It has been far too much for me to manage, and I cannot tell you how thankful I was to see you arrive!"

"I can well imagine," I answered, glancing at Victoria, who watched us like an animal poised to spring.

She tilted her head—as her mother had done earlier—and with determination wrote on the tablet of paper: *I am sorry you have traveled so far, for I do not need a teacher. I can paint without anyone's help—if I want to.*

Her eyes glowed incandescently, her irises growing almost as black as her pupils.

Without hesitation I pulled several watercolors from my leather folder. They were my favorites: a portrait of Father smoking a pipe, a study of a girl selling flowers, and several street scenes of New York in the rain. Though the paint had dried in hard clumps in places, the paintings tried to capture the movement of life.

Victoria studied them slowly. Eva and I exchanged pensive glances, but neither of us spoke. When she had finished with them, the paintings were laid gently on the bed and Victoria scanned my face intently.

She picked up the tablet and wrote: *Who is the man with the pipe?*

I wrote that it was Father, who had died suddenly.

What caused his death? came her query.

It was a heart attack.

A spark of interest lit her face, and she was about to write something more when Eva snatched the tablet away from her. Victoria glared at the maid, her eyes blazing. There was no earthly reason for the girl's hateful look, and I turned away, suddenly chilled.

"Oh, but she is determined," Eva ground out as she wrote that I was to dine with her mother and uncle this evening.

Victoria looked at me and back to Eva and wrote: *You will hate them both.*

"Nasty girl!" Eva furiously motioned to Victoria to go to her play area. "Madam, I think it would be better to end our meeting for tonight. She seems to be unduly excited, and I'm afraid she will not sleep well."

I rose, too, and in silence packed away my pictures. I could not fathom how I would communicate with the sullen, strange girl, but I was moved to great pity. Her condition was more serious than I had imagined, and I was untrained as well as unprepared for a post such as this. Victoria begged for attention, but I knew, instinctively, that I was not the person to give it—nor was Father, were he still alive. I was thankful that he would never know this discouraging and hopeless situation.

With a great feeling of heaviness, I said my good-byes and returned to my rooms. A few minutes later the tall, frail maid came for me, and as I followed her through the gloomy halls to the dining room, I could not deny the emotional battle that raged within me. I needed to find Catherine, I could not live without the munificent salary offered me, and yet what help could I offer that dark angel?

Knowing how necessary this job was for me, I squared my shoulders and decided that I should find some way to understand her. Perhaps in the course of unlocking the key to Victoria's mysterious behavior, I could discover a clue to my sister's whereabouts.

The Haunting of Victoria

Spurred by my new resolution, I stepped inside the glowing dining room that Jobelle had led me to. She bobbed a curtsy to me, and I was left alone in a room that, I feared, must be set for a royal banquet. The expanse of gleaming oak with its four glowing candelbras and delicate china settings was impressive. Lifting my glance from the table, I scanned the whitewashed stone walls on which were medieval frescoes of world maps. An elaborate wooden musicians' gallery had a place in one corner, and above me rose a rough-hewn, timbered ceiling. Though a fire burned brightly in its cavernous grate, I felt a sudden chill. I was thrust suddenly into a bygone era of glory where battle cries sounded across the downs and there was the rasp of steel as swords were unsheathed. This hall, no doubt, had seen kings and bawdy entertainment and strategies of war planned. Though the fret and fury of that distant past had sunk to dust, something of it remained in the shadows.

My skirts whispered along the pale carpets as I moved tentatively toward the table, catching sight of a flicker of motion. I turned quickly and found myself staring at the marquess. He towered above me in his elegant black evening suit, a scarlet rose on his lapel, his thick black hair parted and combed back from his temples. There was something almost terrifying in his grandeur, and I thought, Yes, this is the king in his great dining hall.

Neither of us spoke for a tense moment, and I wondered dismally if he waited for me to comment about his niece.

"Won't you have a sherry?" he asked, going to a glass-and-oak sideboard behind the table.

"Thank you," I said.

After pouring the ruby liquid, he came 'round the table and handed it to me. My hand touched his lightly, and for a strange instant I sensed the leashed passion of this man—stormy, fierce—and I was alarmed. My muscles turned to water. This man's casual indifference belied the steel resolve that was surely hidden from the world. I sipped my sherry, trying to understand what lay underneath his polished veneer.

"I've met your niece, and I hope I can help her," I told him finally.

He smiled, but his eyes were dark.

"She seems to suffer greatly; it's as though she is very scared and quite mistrustful . . . and unhappy." My words of truth sounded almost cruel.

Rothesay stiffened, but his formal manner never slackened. Without warning, he turned to the elaborate table and waved for me to go to the table.

"It seems we have an exuberant staff tonight. I had no idea that the entire table would be set; I hope it will not disappoint you to dine with only myself and Lady Rothesay."

"I am relieved. I would find it rather intimidating to eat at this table when it was full."

He faced me, his mouth mobile, his dark eyes snapping. "Would you? A lady such as yourself must have seen many dinner parties. Especially in that art world of yours."

"I am afraid not," I said, foolishly lowering my lashes. Did I detect a note of mild amusement?

"Tell me a little about yourself," he said suddenly.

I was bewildered by his query, and not a little skeptical. Cautiously I told him that Mother had died when she was young, that Father and I were left alone, and that he taught me to paint. I never mentioned my sister. Did the marquess notice a similarity between us?

He listened to my story with, I thought, a slight air of impatience, and it was not until his eyes lit on the door behind me that I discovered why his attention had not been mine. To my relief, I saw that he had no real interest in my background—or in my sister.

"Ah, here is Margaret now! And how lovely you look, dear."

I turned to behold a woman whom I'd been sure could not get any more beautiful. Yet she had outdone herself. Her glittering gown of blue and pearl could have rivaled that of a queen at a coronation. Her luxuriant red hair was pulled up in a smooth roll, with glittering azure clips, exposing a graceful neck and shoulders; about her neck was a wide band of pearls; her bodice was low and revealing, and from

The Haunting of Victoria

below her tiny waist the dress fell in a cloud of silk and brocade. Her eyes were luminous as she smiled gaily at the marquess.

I felt embarrassingly like an intruder, for the sizzling chemistry between the two was indication that they would rather dine alone.

"Thank you, James." Her voice was low, measured. She turned to me as though I had just appeared. "Miss Durnham, won't this be pleasant? I do so enjoy guests for dinner."

Though Margaret condescended to politeness, I felt awkward and painfully aware of my plain appearance. For a stabbing instant I wanted to emulate her, to know the secret behind her beauty. There was curiosity, envy, and a deep sense of loneliness all churning within me. Did she appreciate how fortunate she was to sit at her own glowing table, to have such a man's admiring attention?

The marquess helped us into our chairs; we fluffed our monogrammed napkins and Rothesay poured the cool claret, turning to me.

"Miss Durnham, I only waited to ask you more about Victoria until Margaret arrived. Now that we are all assembled, I would like to know more about what you think of the girl. Now, please be honest. Do you think you can revive in her an interest in living?"

I was acutely aware that he kept glancing at his sister-in-law. "What if I said I thought I could do nothing?" I answered tentatively. "Would I be turned away?"

A scandalized look passed between them.

"Miss Durnham, I am sorry if that is the best you can do. But this position requires a great deal of courage, and if you feel you cannot help her, then we are no better off than before. Are we, Margaret?" He smiled, but his voice had a steely edge.

"No, James. But, Miss Durnham, tell me why you think you can do nothing for her?" Margaret turned her lovely gaze upon me.

For a moment I felt sorry for her; she had all the glories of the material world—beauty, wealth—but her only child flirted with madness.

"I did not say I could not help her; it only seems . . . a difficult task. It's clear that Victoria is quite ill, but, of course, I have no way to measure how ill she is. Since I did not know her before . . . before her illness," I said, my voice thin.

"Then there may be a chance to save her?"

I glanced at the marquess. His urgent tone belied his calm demeanor.

"I hope so, Lord Rothesay. If I can persuade her to pick up paintbrush and canvas, and if she loves painting as much as you say she does, then perhaps I can spark a flame. My only hope is that"—I sipped my wine, dredging for the words—"communication with her is not too difficult."

"But she can communicate through her art." Margaret leaned forward, her pale skin glowing in the candlelight.

Rothesay's look lingered a moment on his sister-in-law before he turned to me. "There is a tale about a beautiful woman who was struck deaf and dumb when she married a handsome prince and discovered that he was, in fact, really a frog. It was her discovery of this that made her a prisoner."

Margaret's throaty laugh pealed through the air. "What is the point you are making, James? Are you playing philosopher again this evening?"

I was taken aback at her audacity, but Rothesay ignored her and continued. "The young woman was trapped in a cave and eventually her loneliness spurred her into painting. She painted colorful wall murals, and the tragic story of how she had married a man she didn't know was clearly revealed. She grew old, still a prisoner of the cave, and one day a great king stumbled upon her and the remarkable frescoes she had painted. The quality of her work was instantly recognized, her story became well known. Incredibly she was released from her spell, and she became young and lovely again—and could speak and hear again."

"Our sweetest songs are those that tell of saddest thoughts."

My words were barely spoken when Margaret interjected, "What I would like to know is did the prince become a

The Haunting of Victoria 35

prince again or was he destined to remain a frog?"

Her eyes sparkled with humor.

A pause fell heavily upon us. The Marquess bristled, but forced a crooked smile as the tapestried curtain parted and a haughty-looking butler in coat and tails entered and served cold sliced tongue from a silver platter.

"The prince was destined to remain a frog, for in his heart he was cruel and unkind." Lord Rothesay shot a pointed look at Margaret before continuing. "The point I was making is that perhaps Victoria can be cured if her spirit is awakened through her love of art," Rothesay said with aplomb as he pushed his half-eaten appetizer aside.

"Is that what you think?" Margaret asked me.

"I hope so," was all I could offer.

Rothesay was leaning back in his chair, contemplating us. "The day after the American historian disappeared . . . you've no doubt heard the stories or read the news about our tragedy?"

I swallowed hard and choked on a sip of wine. "Yes," I said finally, clearing my throat. "Yes, I've heard about it."

Margaret's long lashes lowered as she rested her chin on her hand. "She was a brassy sort of woman, don't you agree, James?"

His shoulders moved in an indifferent shrug.

"She worked hard, I won't discount that, but she was very forward and liked a lot of male attention. When she disappeared at the All Hallows' Eve party, we . . . oh, we could only surmise that she just up and ran away with someone from town. We never saw her again," Margaret told me as she picked up her glass and drank greedily.

"I suppose that is the only way to account for a disappearance," I said simply.

Margaret raised her brows.

Rothesay continued the narrative in a grim voice. "The next morning Victoria's governess came to us in a highly agitated state. Before she could tell us what had happened to Victoria, she begged to be released from her post."

"James and I raced to her rooms, where Victoria sat with an almost unnatural stillness in one corner. Her look at me was one that caused my blood to . . ."

In a spasmodic jerk, Margaret pulled a lace handkerchief from her sleeve and pressed it against her eyes. Then she picked up the tale again. "It was as though she didn't know me. Her own mother. I tried to talk to her, to comfort her, but she never . . ." Her eyes were glassy with unshed tears. "She hasn't spoken since."

The marquess went to Margaret and covered her bare shoulders with his strong hands. She passed a trembling hand over his. From beneath the layers of their civility and training the bud of hidden grief was emerging. It was a private moment.

I stared at my wineglass, wondering if Victoria's fright and Catherine's disappearance were connected. And wishing fervently that they were not.

"We are sorry to disturb you so," came the marquess's velvety baritone. "We have been suffering over Victoria's situation for six months now, and that is why we are so eager for some sign of improvement."

I met his look. His face looked hard in the candlelight, his eyes dark, even cruel.

"No, I am sorry for you. It must be a terrible situation for you both."

Though I longed to ask more, this was no time to do so. Soon I would have to know the full story about Victoria Rothesay. But first I would befriend the girl, win her trust.

The dinner continued with an unnatural air of lightless. Our conversation touched on superficial topics as we exchanged nods of agreement. As the meal drew to a close with cups of vanilla pudding dusted with sugar and strong tea with steamed milk, I felt that I must be out of the Rothesays' presence as soon as possible.

Margaret and I exchanged good nights, and the marquess rose and walked with me across the room, pulling the great door open. He surveyed me carefully for a moment, and I blushed—maddeningly. Why did this arrogant man unnerve me?

The Haunting of Victoria

I bid him good evening and turned to face the yawning expanse of shadowy corridor. The wavering light from the sconces sent an unnatural illumination to the ornamental chairs and set of war shields along the stone walls. A moan, like the castle sighing, wafted down the hallway, and I shivered involuntarily.

"May I walk you up?" the marquess asked.

I hadn't expected this, but agreed without hesitation when he offered his arm. He gave a reassuring smile to Margaret as we made our way down the hall.

There was a lazy smoothness to his strides, and with skirts flowing around my feet, I skimmed next to him. It felt ridiculously intimate to rest my hand on the arm of such a person. His name had been famous for decades, he should be a relic, a museum piece, not a living, hot-blooded man. And touching the fine cloth of his jacket, breathing in his masculine scent of clean soap and tobacco made my senses reel at his vitality.

Stop, it! I told myself. My sister may be locked away as his prisoner at this very moment.

"This castle creaks and shudders at night, but don't be frightened. It's only the wind 'round the turrets."

His voice riveted my attention. We stopped at the base of a cylindrical stone stairway.

Leading the way, I laughed halfheartedly. "Why should I be afraid?"

He trod close behind me. "Because there are rumors, I'm afraid, of a ghost who haunts the grounds."

We crested the stairs, and I turned to face him.

"Please." He extended his hand toward the corridor that led to my rooms.

"Under my supervision, we are carrying out structural repairs, and with all the commotion of the missing historian and the dusty artifacts uncovered as well as digging about the old prisons in the basement, well . . . many rumors are started about the dead walking again. You know, superstitious people with active imaginations."

We trailed past tapestries and portraits painted by the Old Masters until we came upon the carved door to my rooms.

"Sir, I do not have a frivolous nature." We stopped under the arched entranceway to my room. "Nor do I listen to idle gossip. My mission here is to teach your niece to paint, and the sinking of the old castle will not disturb me. Ghouls and goblins have never worried me, I assure you."

He smiled, his eyes lighting. "I have misread you, and I am sorry. You are quite levelheaded, I can see. More like a man, really. I hope you sleep well."

I was ready to give a bitter retort when he offered his hand for me to shake once again. I put my hand in his and felt the warmth of personal contact. I drew away a little too rapidly, and knew that he was aware of my abrupt gesture.

"Good night," he said, turning on his heel.

"Good night," I answered, wishing he was not so aristocratic and I was not so common.

Chapter Four

AFTER SPENDING A restless night, my mind stimulated with thoughts of the marquess and haunting images of Catherine as his prisoner, I woke to daylight. The leaded windows admitted only a thin, brassy gleam, but when I opened the shutters, a pale sky and streaks of scarlet in the east hinted of a day mild and clear. The air was brisk and it penetrated my thin gown. Hugging myself, I saw the turquoise sea far below and a flock of gulls that wheeled and dived in the distance.

Had Catherine seen this same lonely strip of coastline? If only I could know more about the layout of this castle, some of the historical events that took place here, perhaps I could explore on my own.

There was a sharp knock and the door opened behind me. Jobelle, the lean maid I kept encountering, entered and told me I was to breakfast with Victoria this morning in the schoolroom adjacent to her rooms.

I made quick work of my morning toilette, and when Jobelle came back for me, I followed her back up those stone steps and along another dark corridor. I was taken directly to the nursery. It was a room full of dolls, miniature houses and carriages, Gainsborough hunting dogs, and fancy mirrors in gold curlicue frames, of satin and lace. Yet though the morning sun threatened to burst in, the pink brocade drapes were pulled tight and delicate lilac candles in small china holders lit the room. A fire burned in the brick hearth, which seemed inordinately large.

Jobelle slipped out the door, and I made my way to a

highboy laden with silver dishes. Cutlery, china, and linen were arranged next to a steaming platter of scrambled eggs and tomatoes, warm toast in a wire holder, and a pot of tea and milk. There was no sign of Victoria, so I ate alone, wishing secretly for a cup of coffee.

When I had finished my meal, I began searching through an enormous shelf of books, which contained many of the finest children's classics. One book in particular, which sat on the end of a row, caught my eye. It was thin as a pamphlet and its title was: *Tavistock Castle: Its History and Origins As Set Down by Crichton Stuart, Hereditary Keeper of the Castle, 1802.*

What serendipity! I grabbed the thin volume and leafed through it. There were pencil sketches of the castle—early as well as later floorplans. It was mostly text, and it read as a sort of historical treatise. At the back of the book I was shocked to find an appendix—written by the marquess, with facts compiled by Catherine!

My heart in my throat, I began scanning the material. When Victoria entered, I looked up, trying to subdue my eagerness.

Her thick hair was pulled back demurely with a yellow bow, and she wore a plain knee-length day dress in pale lemon. She looked more sophisticated than the wide-eyed sprite in ruffles I had met yesterday. Standing stock-still, she held me with her stare, and I noted that under her arm she carried a notebook.

"Good morning," I said cheerfully, disappointedly laying aside the book.

She furrowed her brows.

"Oh!" I exclaimed, embarrassed. Of course, she can't hear, I thought wretchedly.

At a loss for what to do next, I gestured toward the highboy still laden with steaming platters. "Breakfast," I said, hoping she would understand.

She merely shook her head and, extending her notebook, began to write something. I watched pensively while she concentrated. It was good that she was at least showing interest in telling me what she thought.

The Haunting of Victoria

But my optimism was soon shattered. She held up the notebook, and from across the room I read the bold words: *I do not want a nanny or a teacher. I am capable of taking care of myself. Go away!*

An ambitious idea spurred me to the door. I signaled for her to follow, but she only watched me with suspicion. She exerted a peculiar power as she stood there like a marble figurine.

I was not deceived for a moment that I was in charge. Still there must be a way to encourage her to come with me. If only I could make her feel that *I* had something to learn from her, that I wanted to know more about the castle in which she lived . . .

I remembered the volume on the history of Tavistock.

"Please," I said, walking toward her, holding out my hand, "can I use your notebook?"

Victoria lowered her long lashes as though she had dismissed me, but seemed to have understood. She shoved the paper and pencil into my hand.

I quickly jotted the message that my interest was piqued by the treatise, and that I wanted to take a walk, see the downs, the sea, and since I was especially interested in history, I would love to see the ruins. Could she take me there?

The girl's face turned chalky, and her lips began quivering intensely as if she were trying to speak. She clutched her bodice and began breathing erratically. I reached for her hand, but she withdrew from me as if recoiling from fire, and tore out the door.

Without wasting a moment, I charged after her. Was she ill? What had I done? At her room I was met with a closed door, and when I reached a hand to knock, I heard banging within.

Obviously she cannot hear me knock, I reminded myself, and turned the brass knob. Thankfully the door was unlocked, and I entered her suite of gloomy rooms lit only by flickering candles and wall sconces. The rose-pink drapes were pulled against the bright day. A pile of discarded baby dolls lay scattered on the floor about her four-poster;

the satin bed curtains were drawn.

With caution I moved to the bedside and pulled open the curtains gently. Inside the murky burrow, sheets and embroidered quilts were bunched up at the top of the bed. An enormous pair of eyes peeped out at me from under the covers.

Moving slowly so as not to frighten the girl, I touched her forehead with my palm. She flinched slightly, yet did not pull away. Her skin felt clammy, but I was relieved that there was no sign of fever.

I regarded her for a moment, then sat on the edge of the bed, the satin draping my head and shoulder. What can I do? I thought hopelessly. What could have startled her so?

I hadn't lied when I told Lady Rothesay that I got along well with children, but my experience had been fairly superficial. What made matters worse, I had come to Victoria, instead of her coming to me for instruction. She didn't need me—as she'd let me know most emphatically—but I needed to be here.

"How unfortunate!" I exclaimed.

She lowered the quilts a little, exposing the rest of her ashen face.

Shall we try again? I queried in her notebook, smiling in spite of my nerves.

She stared at me, her eyes glistening with tears, her lips severe, her nostrils quivering. What was it that she couldn't tell me? If only she would learn to trust me.

Behind me I heard the door close and the sound of footsteps.

"Oh, madam! I thought I could find you here."

I turned to find Eva looking at me, a glint of curiosity in her eyes. Her severe gray dress and wispy hair pulled back into a tight knot made her look more formidable than she had looked the day before.

"It is important to adhere to a schedule with Victoria. And since I did not find you in the nursery having break—" She moved next to me and peered at the girl. Victoria responded with a quick, upward glance at the housekeeper.

The Haunting of Victoria 43

I stood, causing the bed curtain to fall into place.

"What happened? What has made her like this?" Her voice was accusatory.

I was eye to eye with the woman I had begun to doubt was my friend. "Eva, I don't know. I only asked her to take a walk with me, and when she read my note—"

"Did you mention the excavations of the ruins?"

"Well, yes, I did. That I wanted her to show me the grounds, including the ruins, of course."

Eva placed her thick hand on my arm. "Madam, it is the one place we avoid talking about. The master has strictly forbidden it. Victoria takes ill at the mere thought of that part of the estate. Perhaps it would be better if you took the morning off and toured the grounds alone. Victoria will be better by this afternoon, I wouldn't doubt."

And so I was hastily dismissed as though I were an errant child. I waved a reluctant good-bye to Victoria and decided that I would not let hurt pride interfere with my first glimpse of the castle in daylight. With a perfunctory nod I left Eva, vowing to discover what had happened in those ruins to arouse such terror in the girl.

I returned to my rooms to fetch my woolen cape with its fashionable Medici collar—Father's last gift to me—and my plain bonnet. Exiting my suite again, I tried to figure out how I could find the front door.

Instinctively I followed the arched passageway back to the stone steps, which would take me to the main floor. A washed-out sun glowed through high, small window openings, and as I descended the spiraling steps more gray light shone in at the strip of window.

I wandered out into the same lofty hallway that Jobelle had led me along last night until I came upon the pillared entrance hall again. Descending the stairs, I crossed through the ground floor, through the arched anteroom, and pulled the gargantuan door open. A blast of cool, moist air assaulted me.

I squinted up at the blue sky. Marshmallow clouds floated lazily above, and in the distance there was the ricocheting sound of a hammer—metal against stone. Descending the stone steps, I surveyed the courtyard that I had barely seen yesterday. Within the daunting stone walls were patches of brittle, dead grass surrounded by scrubby flower beds. Though winter's visage still covered the land, there was promise that this was a more gentle place in summer.

I faced east and headed under the main gate, toward the Roman ruins in the outerworks. Surely this was where Catherine had been. Would there be any trace of her presence?

A shadow fell across my path.

I glanced up quickly, struggling to see the imposing form of a man that had materialized so dramatically from nowhere. The outline moved to one side and became more than a phantom shape silhouetted against the sun. Though he was not young, he was extraordinarily handsome. His striking red coat, trimmed with braid and buttons, was the uniform of a resident custodian, and it lent him an air of authority. His lined cheeks and the crow's-feet around his eyes only enhanced his look of distinction. The streak of white in his beard contrasted sleekly with his black arched brows and thinning umber hair. His dark eyes were watchful, wary, and when he offered his hand, I noticed that it was the hand of a laborer—blunt, thick, muscled.

"Hello," he said in a deep, resonant tone.

"Hello," I answered meekly as he firmly shook my hand.

"My name is Hal Mathews. I am the gatehouse keeper of the castle. I trust you are the new teacher to the master's lovely young niece?"

Though he spoke with the clipped precision of the British, there was something about his accent that wasn't typically English—as though he were from another country. His overwhelming presence had made him seem at first impression more like royalty than one of the staff.

"Yes, I am," I said.

"I was under the impression that a man was to have come, but it is certainly to my delight that such a lovely young woman as yourself has arrived instead."

"Thank you. I am glad to be here. I have only arrived yesterday," I replied, looking away from his searching gaze.

The Haunting of Victoria

Why explain that my father was dead? He would surely hear my story from the other servants.

"Then, no doubt, you are eager to explore the grounds, see the famous ruins. I will not detain you," he said obligingly, but something in his smooth manner pricked me, and I felt disconcerted.

"I'm on my way to see them now, the ruins, I mean. I know that the marquess is renovating the castle with the help of historians and architects," I said, wondering if he sensed my avid interest.

"Oh, yes. There's been quite a staff here. Unfortunately it's slowed down some since the death of one of the historians."

I faltered. "Death?"

"Oh, I don't mean to scare you. Just that one of the workers disappeared from the site recently. No one knows much about her. She was strange, but a real beauty she was." His smile was reflected in his deep eyes. "Work'll pick up again once winter blows itself out." He glanced up at the calm sky. "I would guess it has finally." He studied me a moment. "Have you been warned?"

"Warned about what?"

He laughed, a rich mirthless chuckle. "An indomitable stone castle perched on an ancient shore, a restless sea tossing below, centuries of toil and pain lingering in the musty walls and ashes of innumerable fires. It stirs the imagination. Does it not?"

I felt my eyes widen. "Yes, it does."

"I'm sorry," he rattled on before I could speak. "I only wondered if you were warned about the ghost that is supposed to roam the grounds at night. Some folks even say they've seen it."

"Oh, that," I said a bit too hastily. When he looked at me sternly, as though I had ruined his tale, I said, "Yes, I have heard about it. A priest, is it? Who is searching for someone?"

He narrowed his eyes.

"Yes, a Spanish priest is searching for a woman who used to live here." He glanced up at a broken battlement. "Many centuries ago. It was during the bloody Spanish Inquisition; he was one of Queen Mary's henchmen, sent to Tavistock Castle to seek out heretics. The young lady of the house was a Protestant. He fell hopelessly in love with her, and when she wouldn't renounce her faith, she was killed. The disconsolate clergyman was never the same again, and his lonely spirit has restlessly searched for Margaret ever since."

Margaret! Briefly I let the alarming coincidence of the name sink in. Mathews tugged at his beard deliberately as though he were appraising the situation. Around us the cooing of pigeons filled the air.

"I hope," I began on far from steady ground, "that this wandering priest does no harm."

He bent toward me. "Not yet. But he is a desperate man. He will stop at nothing to find his beloved."

"I see," I said, deciding that in spite of this man's charm he was as diabolical as Milton's fallen archangel.

The sun passed behind a cloud, and we were momentarily in shadow.

"I'm sorry, madam. I've run on too long and have kept you from your walk. Oh, and don't forget to see the shore." His eyes smiled, though his face remained immobile. It was easy to forget my harsh assessment of him.

"The tide never comes in until late in the day. But if you stroll on the sand, beware of lugworms!"

"I shall be certain to watch my step," I said, unable to hide my smile. *Lugworms?*

"Good day," he called over my shoulder as I moved under the thick, arched gateway.

"Day," I murmured, wondering if the gatekeeper was really one of the marquess's eccentric uncles—hired to entertain guests with colorful tales of old England.

Once through the gloomy passage between the inner and outer gates, I found myself on the ancient bridge that connected the moted castle to the outside world. I blinked at the vista.

Rolling yellowed lawn met the bridge, wide gravel pathways intersected at right angles across the vast terrace

The Haunting of Victoria

where several silent fountains were placed, and in the distance was a lovely old, old church and a crumbling pillar that shot into the air like a projectile.

Just emerging from behind the church was a group of a half-dozen men and women. Dressed in sporting clothes, wearing boaters, and carrying walking sticks, they were led by a dark-suited man who pointed and gestured—he was, no doubt, giving a tour. There was another smaller group of men dressed in rather dreary workclothes who leaned on pickaxes as they surveyed an excavation.

I wandered out across the lawn, past scrubby yew hedges, toward the deliciously decrepit church.

Outside the chapel a handful of lichen-encrusted tombstones thrust out of the barren winter earth, and a majestic beech tree, still leafless, bordered the north wall; the south wall was bleakly desolate except for the first pale blooms of forsythias.

I pulled open the warping door, above which were carved, in stone, signs of the zodiac surrounding a seated Christ. The interior was small and delightfully simple. I took in the clean plaster walls, lancet windows, twisted balusters at the altar rail, but focused on a splendid tomb in the center.

Silently, except for the whisper of my skirts brushing the tile floor, I approached the alabaster sarcophagus. The figures were draped in decorative medieval tunics, their hands steepled in prayer. I reached a tentative hand toward the male figure.

"Has your sister come back yet?" boomed a familiar male voice behind me.

My head snapped around as if I had been shot.

I was face-to-face with the marquess. He rocked back on his heels, his face registering shock and confusion.

We stared at each other for a whirring moment.

"Madam, I am sorry. The party of tourists has lost someone. One of the ladies' sisters wandered off. . . ." He stopped and glanced around the room. His guard was down, there was a chink in his polished armor.

"You startled me. The church was so quiet, and I didn't

hear your steps." I floundered for words, horrified that I trembled.

"I didn't recognize you this morning. Your dress, your hair, you could have been—" His face went tight. "Well, it's my mistake, and I apologize for startling you."

His features were sharper in the morning light, his mouth was drawn in a sneering line, his dark brows frowned above his determined black eyes. His legs were set apart; he exuded arrogance, indignation at my presence. How he had alarmed me with that question, and to my chagrin it was he who seemed dismayed! I really disliked him at that moment!

"I hope there was no harm in touring the church. I was on my way to the seacoast," I said, challenging his insolence.

"Where is Victoria?" His question was brusque, but I had expected it.

"She . . . has taken ill. I wanted her to take a walk with me, but she felt faint and returned to her rooms."

Purposely omitting my invitation to Victoria to accompany me to the ruins, I looked away from him—out the narrow window. He did not stir, and his presence was as heavy as the slab of alabaster.

"I left her with Eva. She's in bed, and I thought perhaps this afternoon, I would"—looking directly at him, I decided to hold my ground—"see her, and perhaps try some sketching."

"Yes, that's a good idea," he said slowly. He was looking past me, at the gleaming tile floor beyond.

I edged by him, and made toward the door. He didn't turn.

"If you see no objection, I would like to continue my walk to the sea."

He turned to face me and raised those dark eyebrows. "Did I suggest that there would be an objection to such an innocent action as touring the grounds?"

"Not in so many words," I said firmly.

He did not answer, but looked puzzled.

Immediately I regretted my bold reply. Was this not, after

all, a man used to servility and acquiescence?

I attempted to retract my statement. "I was not being impudent, sir. It is only—"

"There is no need to explain, Miss Durnham, I assure you. I've had a tiring morning, that's all." He brushed a hand over his face, exhaling a contrite sigh.

"Lady Rothesay has taken to her bed again today, and Victoria's fright at taking a walk is exasperating as well as wearing. And I am the only one to deal with the damned tourists . . ." His voice trailed off drearily.

I was sure he wanted to say more. And for a moment I wanted to listen. But he caught himself, and his tone became blunt again.

"Promise me one thing, Miss Durnham."

"Yes?"

"Do not take Victoria to the site where the archaeologists are digging—or to this church or the lighthouse."

I nodded complacently. What was it Eva had said? The master strictly forbids talk of the ruins?

As if reading my mind, he added, "I can tell you nothing else, I'm afraid. Since I know as little as you do of the girl's malaise."

There was nothing more to say, and a little awkwardly he followed me out the door into the luminous day.

"Thank you for your warning on the girl's behalf. I will need to know all I can in order to help her recover," I said.

A deliberate smile spread across his face, but his eyes remained dark and probing.

I forced a smile in return and walked away, feeling his anxious gaze on my back. How unnerving he could be! No wonder his sister-in-law had taken ill. Was she a bit afraid of him, too, as I was beginning to be?

Crossing the stubby downs to the cliff's edge, down a muddy trail to the sea, I came to the strange tumbled strip of coastline. Yellow-green mud and moss-covered rocks stretched to the foamy line of the tide; in the gleaming aqua water little circular . . . lugworms? . . . burrowed in the sand. Above me, perched indomitably atop the dun cliff edge, was the outline of the old lighthouse, dark against the light expanse of sky.

Though this sublime setting would normally have inspired me to pick up crayon and paper, I was oblivious to its beauty. I could only see the marquess's charcoal hair, cruel eyes, contemptuous mouth. Poor Victoria, who had such a stern uncle. I was beginning to think that he had more to do with her illness than anyone was admitting.

I found my way back to my rooms and gazed out my windows, seeing not the lawns and sea beyond—but disdain in those intense black eyes.

And then Eva came to invite me to lunch with Victoria in her rooms.

Chapter Five

AT HALF PAST six on a spring evening in England, twilight begins tinting the world pink, and in the slackening light everything then fades to gray. The evening air was mild still, and it contained the smell of earth.

Victoria and I were wrapped in our cocoon of work. Tall and straight as soldiers, our easels stood close to the open windows. We stood behind them—backs to the still-gold light that warmed our shoulders—dipping our brushes into paint. Our attention was riveted to a clay pot sitting atop a fringed shawl and containing lemon-yellow forsythia blooms.

We should put away our paints soon, I thought, since the day's brilliance is over. I glanced at Victoria, but she was so absorbed in her work that she paid no attention to me.

The week had been long and disheartening. After our first lunch together, she followed me to my rooms and tried a few charcoal sketches. Pleased, I was sure something I had said or done had triggered this response, but she ignored me. Only once did she look at me as if she wanted to speak, her eyes eager and full of longing. My heart broke for her. She wanted a friend so badly, but she was afraid. I could see in Victoria the young companionless girl I had once been.

I hadn't seen Margaret since the first day, nor had I seen the marquess since our disconcerting encounter in the church. Their strange aloofness didn't bother me, but I knew that Victoria suffered severely from their lack of attention.

That evening the marquess made a rare visit to the schoolroom. I hadn't heard his knock or seen him until he was quite upon us.

"Ladies," he said in a rumbling baritone.

I looked up, flushing at the sight of him. He wore all black. A long jacket with a silver watch chain looped from pocket to buttons, his trousers fit snugly, revealing muscled, firm legs, and I could smell the leather of his knee-high boots.

With perfunctory politeness he greeted me, and I him. A powerful longing swept through me, and abruptly I turned away. How utterly ridiculous and hopeless for me to be attracted to such a man! Trying to get involved in my still life again, I realized that I was too uncomfortable to think about painting. He was too close, and besides, I was concerned about Victoria.

She viewed her uncle impassively at first, then gazed at him with a long-suffering stare. He smiled warmly and moved to her with such rapidity I thought my heart would break with the tenderness of it.

When he stood at her side, he said, "Kitten," so softly it was barely a whisper. He pulled out a pair of steel-frame glasses and placed them on his nose. A tendril of hair fell over his forehead. Turning his chin slightly, he regarded first the painting then the girl.

There was a weighty silence as he stepped away from the easels. He signaled for me to join him next to the hearth, and I felt the girl's anxious eyes upon us.

I turned to him, hoping for the best. There was little to tell except that Victoria was painting every day, that we had fallen into a sort of routine, which consisted mainly of breakfast, lunch, and painting. That we never left our rooms.

"She is very enthusiastic about her painting, and I think with a little more time she will begin to blossom like the new spring flowers. There is something, though. . . ." Why was it so difficult to be direct with this man? I cursed myself for my tongue-tied hesitations.

"What is it?" he asked.

The Haunting of Victoria   53

I met his worried gaze squarely. "I am so happy to see you here today"—I bit my lip—"for Victoria's sake. Look how happy you have made her! She needs more attention like this from you. And her mother." I glanced at Victoria, who watched us fervently.

Quietly I said, "She is lonely. Victoria is still a girl, and it matters very much to her that you and Lady Rothesay pay close attention to her. Perhaps include her in some of your daily activities. Take a ride in the coach with her, introduce her to the tourists—"

"Miss Durnham, have you no sense? She is frightened to death of strangers, of going anyplace that is new. I don't doubt that soon she will be ready for a little more adventure, but not now."

"Then if you cannot take her with you on your errands, why not invite her to dinner? To lunch? She needs you." My words were strong, pleading, and again I felt I had said too much.

There was a cold austere light in his eyes as he appraised me. "Miss Durnham, I don't recall hiring a physician. If I need to be informed about Victoria's physical condition, I can guarantee I will not consult an art teacher!"

I stared up at his imposing figure, into his eyes, darkening with anger. "On the contrary, you hired me not only to teach art, but to inspire in her a reason for living. Those are your words, Mr. Rothesay, not mine." I purposely omitted saying "Lord."

"I don't remember giving you leave to plan her schedule, however," he said hotly.

He was giving way to a passionate temper I had not seen before—only guessed at. I wanted to say, "Don't be a fool," but restrained myself.

"I am not planning her schedule. Only suggesting something that may bring her happiness. Besides, you forget, if you ever knew, Lord Rothesay, that an artist is characteristically sensitive, in tune to those around her. Someone like myself might be able to help determine what Victoria needs."

"I will make the decision as to who will take care of my

niece, who will decide if she is capable of romping about the yard. Do you forget, Miss Durnham, who is in charge here?" he growled.

"Oh, no, I cannot forget that, nor can Victoria. Only a king could make himself more scarce!" My voice was full of venom. "I am only recommending that you spend more time with her."

"I won't hear another word!" His eyes flashed.

"But you must hear what I am saying!"

We glared at one another. Jets of flame in the wall sconces hissed. A sea gull cried shrilly.

Victoria stamped her foot so suddenly that the marquess and I turned away from each other abruptly, shaken and embarrassed.

The marquess shot me a reproachful, malicious look. Victoria's eyes were round as pennies, and I thought for a regretful moment she was going to cry. The marquess quickly went to her and dashed off a hurried message—obviously meant to humor her—for, quite suddenly, Victoria's alarmed look passed, and a gleam of amusement lit her dark eyes.

Hedging tentatively toward them, I said contritely, "Lord Rothesay, I want to say how—"

He whirled upon me like a tiger. "You have said quite enough, madam!"

If my anger had ebbed, his surely hadn't. He brushed his hand hastily across Victoria's cheek, then stomped toward the door, slamming it behind him.

I felt like crumbling. What would happen now? Definitely I would be dismissed.

Foolishly I glanced at Victoria, letting her see the confusion and pain that must have shown plainly on my face.

Going to her side, I tore a piece of sketch paper from her pad and, with a pencil, wrote: *I am sorry that your uncle and I fought. Sometimes when adults discuss something very important to them, they become impassioned, and they argue.*

She read, then grabbed the pencil from me. *Is my condition very important?*

The Haunting of Victoria

I glanced at her hopeful face. *Yes*, I answered. *Very, very important. We all want you to get well.*

She was thoughtful and laid down the pencil when I handed it to her for a reply.

Suddenly the door burst open. The marquess stood on the threshold, his face grim, his eyes moving from my face to Victoria's. In a fleeting moment he regained his dignity and planted his feet firmly. He would not let emotions rule him.

"Miss Durnham, I almost forgot to—" He lowered his eyes, and I wondered if he was nervous. No, not him. He looked at me again, his eyes never leaving mine. "—apologize. Sometimes my temper gets a bit out of control. Will you accept my humblest pardon?"

I caught my breath. "Of course." Crazily my heart raced, and I felt blood pound through my veins.

"Good." He smiled warmly. "Oh, and by the way, there will be a ball for Lady Rothesay and myself. An engagement ball. It will be on the Friday next. Now that you are here to teach Victoria, we thought we should go ahead with our arrangements."

My head felt as though it would explode. Of course, he and Lady Rothesay would be married. Hadn't I seen how in love he was with her? Still, something tore at me; feelings I had never felt before were aroused in me by this strange, enigmatic man.

"We would like you and Victoria to attend. We have invited many people, including some of the local townsfolk. Preparations are already under way in the East Ballroom." He rattled on, his voice sounding as though he had rehearsed the speech. "I think she will be ready for a party like that, don't you?"

He knew very well what I thought, and I wondered if he was being facetious.

But for the moment another thought riveted my attention. How easy it might be for me to meet someone who had been at the All Hallows' Eve celebration last fall—the night Catherine disappeared. This was my first real chance at finding a clue to my sister's whereabouts.

"We will be happy to attend. I know Victoria will love a ball as much as I will."

My eyes slid to meet Victoria's next to me. She watched our exchange excitedly.

"Will there be time to have a dress ordered for Victoria? There is nothing that makes a woman—or girl—feel lovelier than having a new gown to wear."

"I will see that Margaret has one made up specially for her."

I smiled at Victoria, still trying to control my unreasonable disappointment.

"Right, then, that is all." The marquess smiled with enthusiasm at Victoria, his eyes flashing. "Madam." He nodded toward me and walked away.

"Milord," I said to his receding form.

I turned to find an unusually animated girl. Quickly I scribbled news of our invitation and how a new dress was being ordered for her.

Her eyes sparkled mischievously, her cheeks were bright with passion, her eyebrows arched in expectation. It was as if she wanted to exclaim in glee. I only wished she could have.

Without warning she placed her hand in mine and signaled for me to follow. I laughed in spite of a tiny spark of superstitious dread that settled upon me. How rapidly she had awakened from her indolence!

I noticed how pale the light in the room had become, how a wash of silver dusted the deepening day. Grabbing a candle from the mantel to light our way, I scurried after her, wondering where she was leading me.

Through the corridor, down the twisting, darkened stairs, and out into the grand arched, pillared hallway that dominated the keep, I followed her. Victoria did not slow her pace until we came upon a circular hall.

From the hall we entered an opulent room, brightly illuminated from a dozen or so gasoliers that hung from the plasterwork ceiling. Several workmen busily cleaned and inspected lamps that sat on shiny wood tables.

Could this be the East Ballroom, then? I breathed rag-

The Haunting of Victoria

gedly. French doors bordered one wall; saffron couches and Chippendale chairs sat about the room. Woven carpets of pale orange and ivory met the scrubbed tile floor, and on the opposite wall two doors flanked a wall-sized mural.

The workmen's activity stopped as they openly surveyed us.

I nodded, embarrassed. "This is the Honorable Victoria Rothesay, and I am her teacher. Miss Durnham."

One of the men smiled, but it looked like a sneer. "We know who she is, madam. And we've seen you 'bout the place."

"Oh!" I exclaimed. It wouldn't be a surprise if one of them had spied me from the gatehouse door.

Victoria was rushing ahead of me—toward the door across the room. There was an urgency to her steps, and eagerly I followed her to get away from the men's prying stares.

I stepped into the next room. To my delighted surprise it was a picture gallery! It rose two stories, meeting an opaque skylight in the middle of the ceiling.

Surrounding us were paintings I would have longed to see in any museum. Biblical scenes, pictures of life in the Renaissance, portraits of royalty. My eyes swept them all; I was fascinated, spellbound. It took no expert to see that the gallery contained works by artists who were luminaries of their age.

There in the corner, among the gallery of stars, was my father's painting of me as a child. My face was shiny with tears, my hair swirled about my head and shoulders in a disheveled display. The lines of my form, a lace scarf tied around my neck, across my shoulders, and falling down my back kept the viewer's eyes moving; the vibrant colors made this work remarkable. It was no wonder that Father had become famous!

I could not linger long, for Victoria had stopped before a magnificent portrait of a young woman. She kept turning toward me in an effort to get me to join her. I moved to her side and perused the masterpiece.

The subject sat in a regal pose, chest high, arms on her lap, liquid eyes betraying anguish. Her auburn hair was pulled back with an elaborate headpiece, the fur-trimmed gown of deep violet contrasted with her ivory skin, the choking white ruff at her neck was draped with a double chain of glittering diamonds and pearls. Hanging from the imposing necklace was a square diamond as large as the base of an inkwell. At her lace-cuffed wrists bracelets dangled with heavy-looking red, yellow, and green precious stones.

Were these the famous hidden jewels that Gavin had told me about on the day of my arrival? They were certainly exquisite enough to be very valuable.

There was something sad, doleful, almost *familiar* about the young woman in the luxurious-looking dress. What were those wide, painted eyes trying to tell me? When I glanced at the plaque on the frame I exhaled a startled "Oh!" It read: *Margaret Rothesay, Countess of Kent, 1539–1557*.

A tingling spiraled through my veins. There was an unmistakable likeness to the lady of the house. I glimpsed Victoria, who watched me with uncanny interest.

"Your mother!" I mouthed to the girl, who understood, for she nodded in agreement.

How strange that Lady Rothesay resembled a descendant of the family when she had merely *married* into it! Perhaps the master and his deceased brother found marrying a double of the original Margaret intriguing.

"How young she was when she died! Hardly out of girlhood," I said to myself, though Victoria inadvertently leaned toward me as if to hear.

Unexpectedly a wave of fright washed over me. The girl had brought me here especially to see this portrait! What a strange and rather macabre thing to do.

Making sure my fear didn't show, I turned her away from the disturbing painting, and we made our way back to the tower that housed our rooms.

We were both subdued that night as we ate the steaming bouillabaisse Jobelle brought us and afterward sat reading on the warm flagstones in front of the fire.

I should have been heartened that Victoria trusted me

The Haunting of Victoria

enough to show me the picture at all—for that was progress. Yet the true meaning of her action remained a mystery, and I, cautious by nature, could not help thinking there was something strange about her motives.

Turning my attention away from her, I picked up the historical treatise on Tavistock Castle again and began turning the pages. I had scanned the book briefly before, and disappointedly found it to be dry. The sketches of the keep—or White Tower, as it was called—and the outerworks—surrounding walls, gates, lighthouse, and Saxon church—were invaluable, however. It was easy to determine the oldest parts of the keep, and from there it took no imagination to figure out where in the castle historians most likely probed about.

The castle was an irregular square. Four sides of different lengths caused the corners to meet at odd angles. The four turrets, however, were circular. Victoria and I lived in the northeast corner, dubbed the West Range.

Curious, I turned to the chapter describing the picture gallery, but found no mention of the Margaret Rothesay portrait. Again, full of fervent curiosity, I turned to the appendix, wondering what Catherine had, indeed, discovered.

The castle was originally an Iron Age fortress, as I had been told; St. Mary-in-Castro Church was built by the Saxons a millennium after the Romans had left, and in 1089 William of Normandy rebuilt the ruins. In 1180 Henry II reconstructed the castle in order to keep watch on the coast.

I skimmed down the text. My eye caught on something intriguing.

By the early sixteenth century Sir Walter Rothesay had taken up residence in the castle. He had risen from a modest local family to become wealthy as a professional soldier and served as chief secretary to Henry VIII. He came into possession of the lands of the Abbey of Tavistock when the king dissolved the monasteries. With his sudden wealth, Rothesay expanded his newly named Tavistock Castle.

Sir Walter ruled like a king himself, assisting the crown in punishing political prisoners. He was more than a little barbaric and built cells to imprison his enemies. At first the cells, high in the tower of the East Range, afforded the prisoners easy escape. Many lowered themselves through the narrow window with stolen rope; one hapless prisoner fell to his death when his frayed rope broke. After these daring escapes, dungeons were constructed—deep in the heart of the most ancient part of the castle. The "oubliettes," as they were called, were hollows of stone not allowing the prisoner enough room to stand or to lie full length. Though one of Rothesay's desperate captives bored a tunnel from the prisons to the lighthouse, no one ever escaped.

I read on, not a little surprised by the marquess's eloquent writing style.

The king died in 1547, and Rothesay, spurred by the wave of iconoclasm sweeping England and eager to retain his power, converted from Catholicism to Protestantism. This new religion was much more tolerant, and Rothesay's beautiful daughter Margaret grew to womanhood believing in this freer way of life.

Margaret . . . yes, the dates corresponded! It must be she!

According to legend, Margaret had many suitors—but was encouraged by her ambitious father to wed the Earl of Warwick, a powerful man of his time. As his betrothal gift, the earl presented Margaret with a necklace of great value. It was a spectacular chain of priceless stones and contained the third largest diamond in the world—cut from the Cullinan stone. Not to be outdone, the girl's father presented Margaret, as her wedding gift, with bracelets bursting with precious stones—to match her necklace.

I started. The famous family jewels!

Now a shadow fell over the land because, after six short years of Protestantism, the king's son was dead and Bloody Mary was on the throne—to rule as a Catholic.

There was no end to the persecution of Mary's Protestant subjects; no one escaped the terror. The Catholic Church had been losing power for two hundred years, and it was determined to regain its wealth and control over the people. Blood on the block never dried, smoke from victims' stakes drifted all across England, the rack turned and poison was administered.

Captivated by the grisly details, I read on.

Through all this, Margaret held steadfastly to her beliefs, and even though she bore a son, she would not change her faith. She was independent, headstrong, a lover of freedom.

One day the malevolent Father Luis del Rio, sent by the queen, came to Tavistock Castle to ensure that the Rothesays changed their faith to Catholicism. Passionate, prone to bursts of temper, and possessing a vitriolic tongue, Margaret told the priest what she thought of his religion. Father del Rio was not put off by the dauntless Margaret— instead he fell in love with her. He was awed by her beauty and intelligence.

The rest of the Rothesays were willing to renounce Protestanism to save themselves a cruel death, but Margaret would not change her faith.

The priest, with orders to torture and kill Protestants for committing acts of heresy, begged Margaret to relent. He promised her and her family freedom if she would become a Catholic. But Margaret would not yield. Before she and her family were beheaded, however, Margaret sheltered her son with yeomen farmers on the neighboring land and hid her jewels. The priest was so devastated at Margaret's death that he drank a draft of arsenic and powdered diamonds.

I shivered. How horribly cruel life had been in those days!

After a decade, it seems, Margaret's son was restored to his splendid place of residence and the family name was continued. The jewels, however, were never seen again.

Startled by a tug on my arm, I jumped involuntarily. Victoria searched my face with puzzled interest. So absorbed was I in Margaret's dramatic tale that I had forgotten the time. Victoria reminded me by yawning widely and holding up her watch pendant.

"Yes, it is late," I said.

It was already ten-thirty, and suddenly my bones ached with weariness.

I closed the book and was soon tucking Victoria's drowsy form into bed. Just as I was leaving her room, extinguishing the lamps on my way, she gestured toward her pad and pencil.

Though she was sleepy, her message could not wait, and when she showed me what she wrote, I faltered in the silence that engulfed us.

It said: *Someone is trying to kill me! Be careful because you may be in danger, too!*

Chapter Six

I LOWERED MYSELF onto the bed and stared at her incredulously. "Who is trying to kill you?" I asked the silent girl. She was sitting ramrod straight and slid the pad and pencil toward me. I wrote my query.

She stared at my message a moment as though trying to comprehend its meaning.

She began writing. *At night, someone comes into my room from there—*

She gestured to the dark oak door that led to the secret stairway. Yes, the entrance that led down to my rooms and below to the old guardroom and exit.

I nodded. Now I wondered if she would tell me that a ghost appeared. And if she did, I would have believed her. . . .

I can't see the face in the darkness, only a figure draped in a long cape.

I squeezed my hands together and pursed my lips. Could this be true?

The figure walks over to me very quietly— She paused a moment, her eyes searching as if to find the words. *It touches me. I never open my eyes after that. I am too frightened, but I sense that the phantom is still in my room for a long time. And sometimes in the morning I am sick.*

She fell back onto her pillows as if her telling made her weary. Her guileless eyes stared at me, sorrowful, afraid.

I believed her, believed every word, but I tried to keep my face from reflecting the alarm I felt. Who could be scaring this girl, and why? Was her illness caused by these

63

phantom visits and did it have nothing to do with the events of All Hallows' Eve at all?

I grabbed her hand and squeezed it gently. Despite the hot fire that burned in the hearth, her skin felt cold and clammy.

I picked up the paper again.

Victoria, what makes you believe I am in danger? Catherine and I were so different I could not believe that anyone knew I had come searching for my sister. And if no one knew that, how could any harm come to me?

I listened to the hiss of the fire and the distant surges of the sea while she wrote her answer without hesitation.

You have made my uncle very angry today. The last person to arouse his bad temper was Miss Ryce, the historian. Even though he liked her very much. But now she is mysteriously gone. Madam, don't anger my uncle again like you did in the schoolroom.

I read her words, and fear twisted around my heart.

Despite the inner voice that bade me to stop, I wrote: *Are you afraid of your uncle?*

Sometimes. He rages about, you know, and yells at my mother, too. That's why she gets ill so much. Her skin becomes blanched, and she succumbs to stomach pains.

Victoria, I am not afraid of the marquess's anger. It was a lie, and I was reeling more from her revelations than I wanted to admit. I quickly added, *But do you believe that it is he who comes into your room at night?*

Perhaps, she wrote.

Victoria—my hand trembled and I could see that she noticed it—*I can tell that your uncle loves you very much. He has expressed much concern for you, and I find it hard to believe that he would want to do you any mischief.*

Her eyes darkened, and her lips parted slightly as if in frustration.

I don't know for sure if it is he who comes into my room at night, but he has acted very strangely since the historian's disappearance. I have reason to believe it is he, that's all.

The Haunting of Victoria 65

She handed me the pad with a touch of indignation. As I read, it was my turn to become frustrated. I penned: *What reason?*

Things that people tell me.

What people? Victoria, what are you referring to? You must be more specific when you accuse someone of breaking into your room and trying to do you harm!

Everyone. Everyone in the castle knows my uncle was attracted to Miss Ryce, and everyone knows how he blames me for her disappearance.

I was thankful that she could not hear my gasp. I stood, and tried to contain myself.

Everyone knows? Except me. Unexpectedly the violet shadows and yellow lamps were ghoulish backdrops to an unraveling drama full of suspicions and menace.

I wanted to shake the girl to procure some answers. But I knew I must be careful not to show too much, not to act as if warning bells were ringing in my head.

Retrieving the pad again, I wrote as steadily as my hand would move: *What makes you, and everyone in the castle, believe that your uncle liked Catherine Ryce so much? And how could he possibly think you were involved in her disappearance?*

I towered over her, my giant shadow looming upon the wall.

After she read my note, her eyes regarded me with a glimmer of mistrust. What had I said now? I was forever treading on sacred ground.

She was pretty and smart, and liked to talk to him about the history of this place, about the renovations.

I didn't answer when she offered me the paper. She kept writing.

Uncle James never actually accuses me of Miss Ryce's disappearance, but he doesn't trust me. He never laughs or reads to me anymore. He loves Mother, but no one else. He is different now, and I can tell it hurts him to be around me. That's why I've become ill, don't you know? I am being punished for doing something evil to Miss Ryce.

Her face was full of eerie triumph, and I wavered in my

answer. How could a wisp of a girl be involved in such an entanglement? Surely the marquess was not so blind and cruel as to blame Victoria for Catherine's disappearance. He had displayed such tenderness today.

With self-control I wrote: *Do not let others' opinions influence you, Victoria. Whatever your uncle makes you feel, I can assure you that you have done nothing wrong.*

A finger of terror touched the back of my neck. How could I be so sure? Still . . . my questions were unanswered.

Was the marquess ever seen alone with Miss Ryce, did he court her in any way? What indication do you have that he was fond of her?

Victoria's answer came slowly, for after her brief excitement her eyes were again heavy-lidded with exhaustion. I was at fault for selfishly pressing the girl.

They took walks, but mostly they sat in the church and talked. I used to see them there, together. She was very nice. I liked her, too.

She handed me her note with a girlish smile and stifled a yawn.

I read her answer, and my breath caught. The church! The marquess had been stunned to find me there, and hadn't he made a comment about me looking like someone else?

I blinked to clear my vision of the marquess.

Did you talk to Miss Ryce? How well did you know her?

With a heavy hand Victoria wrote: *She talked to me about the English kings that used to visit Tavistock, about the precious jewels that are believed to be still hidden. Just think! Precious jewels, just like a real treasure! She liked me, I think, and we used to walk by the seashore sometimes and look up at the lighthouse.*

I read the note with a shudder and glanced at the girl. Her eyes were half-closed.

With a stab of guilt I pulled the covers up to her chin, whispering good night. Glancing over at a very hard-looking silk settee, I wrote a note asking her if she would like me to spend the night. She agreed happily.

It took no time at all to bring my overnight things to her

The Haunting of Victoria 67

room, and by the time I had undressed and turned low the last lamp, she was sound asleep.

The knocking continued with such persistence that I was pulled out of my heavy slumber. A thin glow of light hovered around the draperies. It was morning already!

Distractedly I sat up and noticed Victoria's empty bed. I pulled on my robe and padded across the floor.

"Who is it?" I called.

"Jobelle, madam, I've brought your tea, and I have an invitation from the marquess."

I swung the door open. She looked amused for a moment, but hid the faint smile. Touching my hair, I realized how tangled it was, how shadowed my eyes must be from my restless night. What a sight I must have seemed.

She sketched a curtsy and, with a note of deference, told me that Victoria had breakfasted already and was in the schoolroom painting. Victoria had informed her that I was here.

A draft from the cold hall touched me, and with a tremor I accepted the hot tea.

"The mistress and master 'ave invited you and Victoria to town with them this morning, and they would be honored if you would join them. The mistress wants to purchase a new dress for the girl. For the ball." She smiled and her gaunt face warmed.

I learned on the doorjamb. What an unexpected summons.

Though surprise must have registered in my eyes, my voice was smooth. "Yes, Victoria and I will be glad to go."

"They will meet you in the main hall downstairs as soon as you and Victoria are ready." She bowed her pristine-capped head and turned away, leaving me to stare after her.

I wasted no time in returning to my rooms to bathe and dress in a deep blue gown of simple straight lines. I pulled my hair back in a coil and attached a sapphire brooch to my high collar. The matching cloak I threw over my shoulders was thin, but something told me the day would be mild. I tied a simple bonnet onto my head and grabbed my gloves and purse.

The reflection that stared back at me was not unappealing, but it was a pale contrast to a woman of real beauty such as the sixteenth- or nineteenth-century Margaret. A straight nose, wide mouth, and almond-shaped hazel eyes made up a plain, if pleasant face. But though I tried to affect a look of confidence, there was no hiding the tense lines that had settled upon my countenance.

I found Victoria in the schoolroom happily positioned behind her easel, working with charcoal. She grinned up at me uneasily when I asked to see her sketch, but made no move to show me. Baffled by her strange secretiveness, I wondered if she was still wound up from last night.

Perhaps her painting was to be a gift for someone, and she wanted it to be a surprise. Perhaps, but . . . some queer feeling told me I was wrong.

Victoria was eager for the outing today, and as she buttoned up her walking boots and I helped her into her coat with a matching lace hat and parasol, I could not deny the excitement that stirred within me as well.

The marquess and Margaret were waiting for us in the great medieval hall downstairs. Filtered sunlight shot through the high windows, drenching the room in a cheerfulness that it lacked on cloudy days.

"We are ready," I said, my voice sounding small in the cavernous room.

The couple rose from the settee, and their particular felicity caused me to fidget uncomfortably with my clasped handbag. Margaret placed her thin fingers on the marquess's arm as if to restrain him, but in a moment he broke away from her touch and moved toward Victoria.

"Miss Durnham, I'm glad to see you and Victoria here today," he said gently while kissing Victoria lightly on the cheek.

"Thank you for inviting us," I said, though no one heard me.

He murmured to his niece, "You are beautiful," and she smiled with infinite affection.

I knew Victoria was responding to the marquess's warm look and touch, though I could have sworn she understood his words.

I heard the rustle of Margaret's silk petticoat next to me, and I turned, catching a scent of honeysuckle. She raised her heavy lids to gaze at me and smiled obliquely.

"Miss Durnham." She nodded politely, but her voice was languid, distracted.

I returned the greeting, finding it hard not to gape at her. Even in her simple emerald brocade walking suit she was stunning.

She stood before her daughter and tugged playfully on her bonnet. "You are looking so well today! So well!"

As Margaret turned around she raised her hand to touch her forehead, and I wondered if she was dizzy. But no one else seemed to notice her gesture, so I ignored my misgivings.

The glittering Cinderella coach waited for us at the door. The deep sky was cloudless, and as the marquess helped us into our seats an anticipatory mood seem to infect us all. We sped over the rutted cobbles, toward the gatehouse.

I glanced up toward those Georgian windows and saw Hal, the gatehouse keeper, watching us. As soon as he caught sight of me, he retreated into the shadows, but the imposing figure had undoubtedly been him. I reeled back into the security of my seat and hoped the others did not notice my shortness of breath. There was something diabolical about him, and I could not shake off the feeling that if any danger would come to me, as Victoria prophesied, it would come from him.

With effort I tried to concentrate on the scenery rolling past the windows. Though the countryside had barely changed in a week's time, there were touches of green in the fields and buds clung tenaciously to the trees in the coppices.

On the way my employer told tales about his childhood in the seaside town, and how it had recently grown into a popular resort. I was relieved to see that he especially drew out Victoria by writing down everything he said, even though the bumps along the way made writing difficult.

The horses slowed as we made our descent toward the russet roofs of Dover, and the marquess turned to me. "Miss Durnham, I've been thinking—" Margaret turned a keen ear upon him as he pulled something flat from inside his pocket. "I would like to give you something that may aid in your understanding the history of the castle, a little of our family's background. Perhaps it will be a help with your work." I heard nothing else, for he presented me with a leather-bound copy of the same treatise that I had read last night!

How presumptuous of me to have taken the book from Victoria's room! The blood that flamed my cheeks and the rapid thumping of my heart were an embarrassment, and I wanted nothing more than to flee.

Should I tell him that I had read it already, that his introduction was fascinating? My swift glance at Victoria told me that she found my predicament amusing, but I could tell she would not give me away.

"Thank you," I said unevenly, accepting the book.

"James has written the introduction," Margaret said suddenly, tossing a sharp look at the marquess. "He wants you to read that, I'm sure."

"I will. I'm sure it's . . . very interesting," I said.

I lowered my head, keeping my eyes on the book to hide my reaction. When I glanced up, the marquess was watching me intently.

Hastily I smiled, and he grinned briefly in return. There was an instant of heightened awareness, as though a vague current of emotion passed between us. As soon as I noticed this, it passed, and the carriage was stopping outside a tightly packed line of shops. I tucked the small book safely into my handbag.

When the marquess helped me out after the others, I stepped down so quickly I nearly lost my balance. Laughing, the marquess held out a strong arm to steady me.

"I'm afraid the bright day and fresh air have made you giddy," he teased.

"Possibly," I said evasively. "But I'm so happy that you've invited Victoria out as I suggested."

It was a fumbling effort to distract him from referring to my unsteadiness, and to my dismay he became defensive.

"Margaret and I have planned to take Victoria to town for some time. The opportunity just hadn't arisen yet. We thought it would be a special treat for her to buy a ready-made gown instead of employing her seamstress."

"I'm glad," I answered, but the spell was broken.

Victoria gleefully pointed to an ancient Tudor shop, and we followed her inside. With a painted ceiling, polished columns, gilt mirrors lining the walls, and elaborately decorated dressing screens, the shop was obviously designed to echo the elegance of customers' homes.

We were offered sherry from a butler's silver tray, and Victoria, Margaret, and I were whisked into a private room to examine dresses. The abundance of material indiscriminately spilling off the racks was overwhelming: organza, lace, and satin, moiré silks, taffeta, all in fashionably bold colors. There were tea gowns, day dresses, dressing gowns, with cloaks and capes and hats to match.

There was only a small section of dresses for girls, and the choice was limited, but Victoria found a lovely full-sleeved gown with a high lace collar. She and her mother were taken to a fitting room, and I sauntered back out into the front of the store where the marquess waited.

A trio of musicians was playing softly on a raised gallery. A group of interested shoppers spoke in whispered tones to a smartly dressed salesgirl, and I found a display of fashionable Parisian hats on a far table. Carefully I sorted through them. To my alarm, the marquess came up behind me.

"You must be aware of Victoria's improvement even in a week's time," he said quietly. "Don't think that I am unaware of all you are doing. You have brought something into the house that we have not felt since . . . not for a long time," he finished distractedly.

I was examining a feathered aqua toque as I turned halfway around to look at him. Though the words he spoke were grateful and kind, his gaze was remote. He seemed very far away; it was as though he visibly withdrew himself, but then he shrugged and looked directly at me.

"I believe Victoria likes you very much, trusts you. It is as I had hoped."

"Yes, she is doing better, much better, than when I first met her. But it was not wholly my doing. She is a dynamic young girl and only needed encouragement to come out of her shell a little."

"You are too modest, madam. It is completely your doing, and I—we—both thank you."

I nodded quickly, laying the hat aside. He stepped smoothly past me and picked it up again.

"It would look lovely on you."

I was furious that my cheeks blazed with color for the second time that day, and my throat went dry. I could think of nothing to say.

"Do you have a gown this color? You will need something pretty to wear, too, you know."

Though his tone had not changed, his eyes became warm, a silky light touched them and they sparkled dangerously. I turned away, trying not to read their meaning. He seemed to have forgiven me for my brazen behavior yesterday, but was there something more he left unstated? No, of course not. And yet . . . and yet.

I smiled bravely. "It is a beautiful hat, but unfortunately my gown that would match it is a bit too plain, more of a tea dress really than a ball gown."

I thought that was the end of it, but his next comment was so earnest that I studied him to make sure he wasn't joking.

"Then you must have the dress altered, since the hat is my gift to you."

Before I could summon a no-thank-you, Victoria burst through the draped doorway of the dressing rooms in a gown dripping with lace and ribbons and ruffles. It was much too big for her tiny frame, and it looked as if she wore a curtain.

I laughed and clapped my hands, not knowing if I felt relief or regret at her interruption. I exclaimed over the lovely material, and the marquess held a hand to his cheek and shook his head, his face creased in a smile.

"Kitten, with several yards removed you'll be an enchantress!" He nodded to the hovering saleslady. "Get her proper measurements and have it altered. We'll take the dress. I can see that she will not be happy with another one!"

The earnest clerk beamed excitedly. "Yes, sir. And how soon will you need it?"

"In a fortnight, please. There is a ball that we shall need it for."

His last words were flat, and as the clerk assured him that she could have the gown ready in that time, I glanced at the marquess.

He became suddenly taciturn and still. I followed his unhappy glance and saw Margaret leaning in the draped doorway, fanning herself. She was pale, and her eyes had a glassy sheen. When she caught the marquess's intense look, she steadied herself and smiled lasciviously.

I was so embarrassed by their silent exchange that I said awkwardly, "She's beautiful."

"Mmmm? Yes, she is lovely. But a bit under the weather still, I am afraid."

Victoria, having gotten her way, skipped back into the dressing room, pulling her hesitant mother and the eager salesgirl behind her.

We watched them retreat.

"Is she ill often?" I asked. "Victoria told me last night how her mother takes to her bed often." Because of Rothesay's temper, she had said.

"Margaret has rarely been indisposed before, but since Victoria's illness she has not been well. She's so consumed with worry for her daughter." His face was grim, as though a gate had suddenly closed on his feelings.

"I'm sure it has caused her much distress," I said.

"I don't believe we've told you about Margaret's background." He slanted a worried look down at me.

It wasn't what he said so much as how he said it that startled me. "No, I think not," I said.

"She was married to my elder brother, Ninian Rothesay." He gleamed a smile, but there was no mirth in his eyes. "He was a scoundrel; worse than I, I believe."

"I see."

"Somewhat of an adventurer, he had planned to marry his sweetheart and sail 'round the world. He was quite a yachtsman really, and sailing seemed to be all that mattered to him."

"He met Margaret—Clavell was her maiden name, her father was an actor—at a ball. Captivated by her beauty, Ninian eloped with her—much to the chagrin of my since-departed mother. She hadn't the wealth or social standing that Ninian was expected to, well, marry." He lowered his thick lashes and gently toyed with the hat that he held in his hand. His fingers were long and shapely, but blunt at the ends, muscular, manly.

"Margaret gave birth to Victoria within the year, and three months later the little girl was deposited with my mother for safekeeping while the carefree couple sailed off to the South Pacific."

"Oh!" I exclaimed. How impossible to imagine the pampered Margaret foraging in the wilderness, far from the comforts of civilization.

"She claims that her health problems are partly due to many years of relentless sun, inadequate food."

"It would seem a possibility."

"They were shipwrecked for almost a decade. Though the natives were gentle to them, life was rough and hard. Ninian finally succumbed to a fever, and Margaret, miraculously, found her way back to England when a merchant ship from America landed on Bora Bora in search of spices."

"She spent a year in America, incognito, trying to recover her 'ruined beauty,' she says."

Yes . . . she couldn't lose her beauty, I thought.

"The sun had creased her face, and she was too thin."

I smiled. "I find it hard to imagine Margaret looking bad, no matter what the circumstance."

He bit his lip, and "Vanity, perhaps," escaped like a sigh. But I heard it.

"And all this time Victoria lived with your mother?"

"Victoria has always lived at Tavistock, but not always with Mother. Unfortunately, a year after Victoria arrived, my

The Haunting of Victoria

mother died, and since there was no Ninian—or Margaret—in sight, I came into possession of Tavistock and legally adopted Victoria."

A stormy look tortured his features. Had his brother's loss so disturbed him? Or was he raging at the unexpected demand that he care for a child?

Before I knew what he was about, he signaled for one of the clerks and handed her the hat. "Please wrap this," he told her.

"I will pay for it," I said abruptly, but he caught my arm when I tried to move away.

"No, you won't. It's a gift."

It was impossible to turn away from his powerful inspection, and I felt the warmth of his hand through the wool and silk of two layers of my clothing. "We will settle this account later," I said under my breath.

He released me, but didn't move away. "My motives are completely selfish, Miss Durnham."

I met his warm glance unwaveringly.

"You have done us a great service already, and this is only a token of our gratitude."

There was a sudden commotion behind us, and the marquess and I whirled around to find Margaret leaning heavily on a buxom attendant as the woman led her toward the door. Victoria scampered behind them, a look of horror on her face. For a moment I stood shocked and frozen, unable to move.

Margaret's head was hanging down, wisps of thick hair trembled around her unnaturally pale temples, her eyes were closed, and she gasped involuntarily as though she couldn't breathe properly.

The marquess was at her side immediately, and though I couldn't hear his conversation with the clerk, his face creased into a terrifying grimace. I caught up to them and laid a protective hand on Victoria's shoulder.

"Madam, madam!" A young salesgirl caught up to me and thrust the master's cane and hat into my hands. "Please, if you would carry these. The packages will be delivered to Tavistock."

I thanked her and heard the marquess's urgent voice from outside the open door. "Miss Durnham! Victoria, hurry!"

The ride home was silent and rife with tension. I held Victoria's trembling hand in mine and with a mingling of embarrassment and pity tried to keep from staring at Margaret, who sat across from me. The marquess wrapped a protective arm around her, but she sat forward, holding her head in her hands and moaning occasionally. It was my first glimpse behind Margaret's cool, aloof mask, and her undoing was troubling, to say the least.

The marquess was stiff and uncommunicative, and not once did he glance at Victoria to see if she was faring well. After all, it had been her day. But of course, something as frightening as Margaret's sudden illness took precedence.

Once we reached the castle's main entrance, the Rothesays took their departure rapidly, leaving Victoria and me to find our own way inside. Not until I was delivering Victoria to her rooms did I realize how thoroughly shaken I was.

My hands trembled as I helped Victoria out of her coat and bonnet, and when Eva came to ask if she could bring lunch, my voice quavered.

Victoria retreated into her protective shell, and when I made a feeble attempt to comfort her by writing that her mother would soon be fine, she threw herself on the bed and cried as though her heart would break.

Chapter Seven

THE RECOLLECTION OF the scene in the shop stayed with me during the long days that followed—it had been too vivid to be dispelled easily. No doubt it lingered with Victoria, too, for she was restless, and more than once asked me on her paper if her mother was all right. I could only tell her what Eva had related to me. That the doctor had visited and Margaret was doing much better.

Our days fell into a pattern, and though my time was spent with Victoria, I was eager to search the castle alone. Having my own copy of the treatise on Tavistock only whetted my appetite, and I studied its pages, its maps, thoroughly. I wanted to explore the East Range, the oubliettes, but I could not break away from my responsibility to Victoria. Not yet.

In the mornings we'd closet ourselves in the schoolroom together. She had proceeded from the mysterious charcoal she had been sketching to the actual painting, which she never showed me, and I made a wild attempt to convert my plain turquoise dress into a sort of evening gown. I had no skill as a dressmaker, and several times Eva helped turn a seam for me, and assisted in attaching the silk brocade underskirt. I was hoping the marquess would not give me the aqua hat we had argued over, and since I hadn't seen it since the day in the shop, I relaxed a little, thinking it had probably been forgotten.

Downstairs there was a whirlwind of activity. An exuberant staff whipped the castle into a polished splendor. Furniture was shifted and dusted, menus were planned, paintings moved about to show off the better ones to their advantage. The fine Herend china was brought out to be cleaned, porcelain masterpieces from Meissen were set out, a marble cistern was displayed in the front hall, and the East Ballroom became a room in a Hans Christian Andersen fairy tale.

I can imagine a castle steward, wearing fine robes trimmed with fur, overseeing these cleaning operations, I wrote to Victoria as we left the ballroom one afternoon and headed back to our rooms.

She was subdued and made no reply. Back in our rooms she became ghastly pale and, within only a few minutes, doubled over with stomach cramps. Panicked, I help the girl remove her stiff petticoats and tucked her into bed.

I'm going to find Eva and ask her what to do, I wrote, and the look on her face, wrenched with pain, worried me.

Was her illness chronic and hereditary? It was doubtful. Though I had no medical training, I'd read enough about the properties of morphine and opium to know how similar Victoria and Margaret's symptoms were to someone using excessive amounts of either drug. But why would they? Unless the drugs were administered without their knowing. I faltered at the thought. *Poison?* No, don't be ridiculous. Who would want to harm Victoria and Margaret?

There was of course, no answer for this, and soon I found Eva in the lower quarters overseeing the cleaning. Quickly we made our way back to the ailing girl.

The room was close; a thick, heavy stench hung in the air. Victoria had been sick on her counterpane, and I made a disagreeable face. My aversion gave way to a throbbing pity when I looked at the girl. She sat stiffly against the silk-covered headboard, her eyes round and dark, her skin white as chalk.

"Poor girl, it's all right, it's all right," I gushed, going to her, feeling her feverish forehead.

I pulled off the soiled bedspread and fluffed up the pillows behind Victoria while Eva threw open the shutters.

"Bless the Good Lord, let's get some air in here," she said.

The Haunting of Victoria 79

Eva came to Victoria's bedside and shook her head. Victoria watched us fervently, ashamed, as if she would cry. I knelt down next to her.

Dear, do not worry. Rest, and let us take care of you.

My words penned messily on a scratch pad seemed to reassure her, and she dropped back against the cushions with a heavily drawn sigh.

"I'll fetch some more Londonderry water to flush her system. It's the only cure for improving her digestion," Eva said.

I grabbed her arm. "Eva, is she sick so often? You act as though this is a common occurrence."

"Miss Durnham, it is a common occurrence. She gets sick regular 'bout once a week, and stays limp and withdrawn for twelve hours afterward. Victoria is not just emotionally ill, but physically ill as well." Her silver eyebrows arched. "Don't look so worried, madam. It'll pass, and it's really nothing serious."

"Isn't it?" I queried.

"Madam, what are you getting at?" She crossed her arms over her buxom chest and turned a rather disagreeable gaze upon me.

"I don't know. I can't put my finger on it. It's rather like a premonition or something. If the girl gets sick in the morning . . . and today, after lunch . . . it must be something she ate. Wouldn't that be the logical explanation?"

She shook her head. "You ate the same lunch, did you not? And how do you feel?"

"What about her hot cocoa?"

"Madam, I made cocoa myself today because Cook was busy with preparations for the ball. I can't say what you're getting at, but if you're insinuating that someone laces her chocolate with a sedative or something, you are very wrong."

"I never said that," I returned quickly.

She glared at me. "But you implied it. Now, if you'll excuse me."

Her disapproval of me in that moment couldn't have been stronger. She was in no mood to brook opposition, and she turned away, disappearing out the door to find the bottle of springwater.

I sat next to Victoria again, holding her hand until a light rain began to fall without. Its soothing pattering lulled the troubled girl to sleep just as Eva returned with a quart of water.

In spite of her earlier bad temper, she smiled at the slumbering girl and set the heavy bottle onto the mahogany bedside table. The silver chimes of the little ormolu mantel clock confirmed the hour of three, and I closed the shutters while Eva made up the fire with the logs and threw dried herbs on it.

I turned to her. "As long as Victoria is sleeping, I'd like to walk about the castle. I haven't had time to take a real tour yet."

She nodded her head noncommittally.

"I won't be long," I reassured her as I made a hasty exit and escaped to my own rooms.

There I procured my copy of the treatise, a small gas lamp—calculating that its light would be stronger than and not so apt to extinguish as a candle—and throwing on an old cape to prevent chills from the drafts in the ancient corridors, I set out to explore.

Consulting the map contained in the book, I headed toward the East Range, where the earliest cells had supposedly been constructed—although it was lunatic to think of the possibility of Catherine being held a prisoner in some dank place. But more than my belief in actually finding Catherine, I thought I might find a room that she had searched. Maybe she had left a personal item behind . . . or had she stumbled upon the infamous family jewels?

First I mounted the cold stairway in the polygonal tower that Victoria and I were housed in, reaching the summit of the building. The rain was a velvety, fine mist, and fog, thick as soup, gathered about me. I stood a moment, touching the cold stone battlements, and heard the rush of the sea and sea gulls' cries in the distance. How I would have liked to view the countryside and the seacoast below me! But I hastened on.

I kept the book secured inside my cape and held tenaciously to the lantern. Walking carefully along the paved parapet—worn, I was sure, by centuries of trampling—I tried to calculate which way the sun rose.

"East, east," I said aloud, turning to my left.

A film of cloudlike smoke swirled and abated momentarily, allowing me a panoramic view. I glanced around excitedly and for a split second saw what looked like a flicker of flame just ahead of me. I looked again, but the light was gone. Could I have really seen it, or was it my exuberant imagination?

I headed toward the phantom light and came upon a dark slab of nail-studded door. I pushed. To my amazement, it gave without hesitation, and I stepped into a darkened interior. Holding my lamp high, I saw that I stood in an entrance hall. High, leaded windows admitted a thin wash of light, and on the stone walls were deteriorating sections of what was once probably a magnificent wall painting. I went closer to look.

Figures of saints were depicted against a background of the leopards of England and fleur-de-lis of France. Much of it was dulled, and many parts were missing entirely. The room contained no furniture, and except for the painting, it was of the sternest character.

There was a door and a movable wood screen on the far wall. My heart pounded as I approached the door and pulled the bolt. It moved with a shriek that echoed eerily through the hall. The sound seemed to go on forever, winding back through the dark, deserted passageways. Nervously I glanced behind me. Would someone come soon and catch me in this bleak corner?

Finally the door budged, and with a stumble I crashed into a small closet with a high, open hole for a window and two toilet seats! It was a feudal latrine! I backed out of the cold room and felt a sticky substance cling to my head. I batted wildly at the spiderweb and closed the door behind me with a bang.

I inhaled sharply and began to shiver. Was it worth tripping about a deserted tower to find a piece of Catherine's puzzle? I steadied myself. Yes, it was. I had traveled a long way to be here, and now was my chance to find something. Anything.

To my amazement the decorative screen was covering a small landing at the head of a wide flight of stone stairs. I descended the winding steps until I came to the ground floor, or was it the cellar? I came to a timbered circular room with arched anterooms built into the wooden walls. I peeked into one of the little rooms. There was a vaulted roof and a hearth in the corner. I had read earlier that guardrooms designed like this were positioned above the treacherous dungeons.

Across from me was an arched entranceway filled with darkness. With fear in my tread, I walked to it. A narrow, grim-looking staircase wound down farther than my light would illuminate and seemed to end at the bottom of the earth.

I crouched down, placing the lamp on the ground and keeping my puffy skirts away from the fire, and referred to my book. I skimmed to the chapter on dungeons and oubliettes.

I read aloud, my voice sounding unnaturally loud.

"Father John Gerard, who was tortured in the dungeons to extract a confession of treason to the king, built the infamous tunnel leading from his cell to the lighthouse. Though the tunnel was successfully completed, he was captured by one of Rothesay's men and locked into another cell, where he died in frustrated despair.

"His account reads: 'I was led through a subterranean passage lit by candles. It was a place of immense extent. In the room were arranged divers sorts of racks and instruments of torture. I was led to a great upright pillar of wood and strung up for an hour, my hands clamped in the irons. The pain made me faint, and when I awoke, that beast Rothesay demanded a confession. When it was not forthcoming, he shouted, *"Hang there until you rot."* ' "

I shut the book. A whisper of sound made me stop breathing for a moment. Was that a footfall? My senses were alert, vibrating. It seemed reasonable that I was peering down the stairs that led to those cells.

The Haunting of Victoria

I stood and descended the first steps cautiously. My light flickered and wavered for a moment, and I stopped and held my heart. Was there a draft? The flame steadied, and I continued down the narrow, steep stairs. Having counted at least seventy-five steps, I set foot on the bottom.

The air was suffocating and close. I held my lantern high and the movement caused it to dim. This was definitely the subterranean passage I had read about. I moved to the interior, seeing that the ceiling was vaulted and supported by stone pillars. Not until I crossed to the far wall did I realize that this room was more than a cold, empty place.

There was a large square frame made of rotting wood. Inside were two wheels, a narrow one at the top, with two iron chains attached to it, and a bottom wheel.

"Ohhh!" I screamed, almost dropping the light.

It was undoubtedly a torture rack from the sixteenth century! Next to it was a ponderous square block with a curved indentation on top. Could it be . . . no, not the block where prisoners were beheaded!

Dear God, what a terrible place, I thought. Goose bumps rose on the back of my neck. If there was a ghost of a long-dead priest, surely he would haunt these chilling corridors. Had the first Margaret died here under her father's own roof, or was she taken to the much-feared Tower of London?

"How awful," I whispered to the slick walls.

I turned from the grisly devices and blundered into a huge mechanism that looked like a log with ropes and chains attached. I scanned it with my light. The ropes were wound around the midsection and reached up into the dark vault of space above me. On either side of the log, large supporting poles were attached. It looked as if these supports enabled the log to roll and the rope to be wrapped around it. What macabre use had it served? No doubt another kind of torture.

Behind the archaic instrument was a gaping hole, and with extreme caution I stepped around it and into a dank chamber where I could not stand. I knew at once where I was. A ghastly warmth engulfed me as if a thousand lingering spirits exhaled a communal choking breath.

The walls and ceiling seemed to close in on me, and I swayed dizzily. Touching the wall's damp indentations, I made out a crude carving: *WE*. Part of a sentence or a name scratched by a hapless prisoner, perhaps . . .

Another gust of air hit me like a blast and I turned abruptly to leave. How fearsome was this devil's lair and how foolish to have come here! There was no trace of my sister, and if any jewels had been hidden, someone a long time ago must have searched here—a most probable place.

Suddenly, as if hell itself opened, I heard a wailing squeak and moan from high above. My first impulse was to run, but before my muscles could move, an enormous iron sliding gate with spiked edges crashed down in front of me, missing me by a hair.

I was crouched in a boneless huddle, and my light wavered wildly. It took a few seconds before the horror of my situation dawned on me.

Someone had followed me, someone was watching me, waiting to strike. This had been planned.

Someone is trying to kill me, and you may be in danger, too! Victoria's awful words came reeling back, and I thought for a moment I would faint.

How stubborn not to have believed her words, to have attempted such a foolish search of the castle! Now what had I done?

"Hello!" I called. "Is anyone there?"

Only a thick airless silence fell on my me. I peered through the ancient gate. There was not a stirring in the darkness, as though life itself had been snuffed out.

"O God," I whispered. "Help! Can anyone help me!"

The sound of my voice came ringing back to me, as if I spoke inside a tunnel. I must quell my rising panic, I tried to reason, for if I lost my good sense, I would surely be . . . down here forever.

There must be a way out, even a logical explanation for this. The gate had not been touched for centuries, and

The Haunting of Victoria

my movement caused it to come loose, even if I didn't touch it.

Placing the lantern on the floor, I heaved at the gate from its bottom. It didn't move. I tried again, and again. But the unwieldy piece was immobile. Then I saw with accelerating dread that the gate was fitted into grooves in the floor to prevent passage.

"What can I do? What can I do?" I asked, turning about.

It wasn't difficult to understand the incurable despair prisoners of long ago must have felt. But I was not a prisoner! I would get out of here soon. Someone would find me. After all, I had told Eva I wouldn't be long ... and Victoria would miss me.

Still, would they think of looking here? It was a very unlikely place. How long would their search take, if, indeed, there was a search?

Finally I sat on the cold flagstone floor and wrapped my mantle around me. The terrible doom seemed to suffuse my bones, and I wondered if I might go mad or suffocate to death. My skeleton would rot and my soul would join the others in immortality. Frozen fear gripped me as I shook uncontrollably.

Never in my life had I been so close to hysteria. I covered my mouth to suppress a sob, wondering what the time must be. Ten minutes could have passed or twenty-four hours; I could not begin to guess.

I stood for a while and paced, but there was no room and my back ached with hunching. Was it dark yet, was everyone busy with evening chores? No one would think that I was actually missing.

Missing ... oh, this must have been Catherine's fate, too! From Father's description, I visualized the laughing, outgoing woman optimistically reassuring the marquess that it would behoove him to investigate the cellars. Father had sketched a clear picture of her insatiable curiosity. It followed then, that she would poke around these pestilent dungeons for a clue to the hidden jewels. And she had found many clues to Tavistock's history before she vanished. But someone didn't want her prowling about. She could have been locked up here . . . and then?

I started. Was that a noise? Yes, it was! Unmistakably footsteps! I didn't move, my eyes riveted to the inert darkness beyond my pool of light.

"Madam?"

A burst of light appeared in the room, and a dark figure materialized. I sobbed out an exclaimation of joy and relief. To my amazement, I was looking into the marquess's frightened face!

"Miss Durnham, are you all right?"

"Yes, yes, I am fine!" Though I trembled all over, I tried to maintain a modicum of composure.

He held his light up and searched my face. "You were not hurt when the gate came crashing down?"

"N-no." How did he know what happened?

"Good. If you have patience for another moment, I will raise this blasted portcullis and get you out of there!"

He turned his back on me and twisted and turned some levers. I noticed that he was elegantly dressed in black evening clothes and wondered how he could have come to find me if he were busy with guests.

He swore angrily under his breath and wrestled with a giant pulley, which moved agonizingly slowly. The gate was raised, and I stumbled out, so eager that I almost fell.

He caught my arm and steadied me. But instead of releasing me, he gripped my arm tighter and leaned close, the flame of his candle lighting his dark eyes, heightening his grim expression.

"For God's sake, lady, do you know how dangerous your little trip might have been?"

"Yes . . . yes, I think I can see that."

"It would have served you right if I had left you trapped! You've no right to go slinking around in forbidden parts of the castle!"

I stared at him, disbelieving.

"Slinking around? I merely took advantage of a quiet afternoon to see if I could find a clue to . . . why Victoria is so emotionally ill. I only assumed that—"

The Haunting of Victoria

He silenced me curtly, his face pinching into a grimace. "Assume nothing. Not at Tavistock! Don't you realize how foolish it is to wander about, unchaperoned, in clearly uninhabited sections of this place? You are surely taking your life in your hands, and you may not be so lucky a second time."

I gasped, trying to gather my wits, and for the first time felt how firmly his hand was clamped on my arm. My ire was rising.

"I wish you would tell me why you are so indignant when I am the one to have just escaped a brush with death! And you may let go of me now. I won't run away."

He released his grip, but I still felt the burning of his clasp on my arm. No doubt he had left a bruise.

"You are a fool, madam, to ever have risked coming here! Will you please follow me? I will take you to the safety of your rooms and have tea sent."

His blazing anger relaxed a little and he slipped his arm through mine. Still dazed and on the verge of tears, I allowed myself to be led away from the dire cell that I would never visit again. Leaning close to him, I didn't fight the sense of security he made me feel.

Past the dank and moldering walls, up the turning stairs, we walked, and I didn't notice that he was taking me a different way back to the West Range until we came to an enormous room I'd never seen before. I followed him across the entire room until we reached the far side, where there was an exit. Stone walls with high, tiny windows and a grim tile floor made the room seem like another torture chamber, and I shuddered.

The room was filled with weapons, and the armor of soldiers was arrogantly displayed on dummies. On four walls were wicked-looking lances, spears, and knives with carved handles. There were ornate guns of all shapes and sizes and a treacherous-looking cannon sitting in a corner.

For a horrendous second I feared he might remove a gleaming knife from the wall and plunge it into my chest. Suddenly I could not trust the man who had magically found me, reasoning that he could not have known my whereabouts unless he had followed me. And had dropped the gate on me!

He turned to me at the dark aperture that led out again.

"These are the famous armories that you've perhaps read about." His tone was severe, as if he were unwillingly giving a tour.

"No, I don't think I've heard of them."

He kept walking, and I hurried to keep up, glad to be out of the gloomy room.

We were back at my rooms in a very short time. He didn't enter, but remained in the doorway, as if the conversation was not over yet.

I turned a defiant look upon him.

"I will tell Eva to send tea up immediately." He paused and looked down. "I'm sorry for this. I can tell it has caused you a great deal of anxiety."

"Yes, more than you can imagine! Sir, before you leave, can you tell me how you knew what happened?"

He met my gaze levelly. "It has happened before."

"Wh-who else was trapped there?" I rasped.

"The historian who has since disappeared. She was measuring the foundation, trying to estimate some dates, when the mechanism broke loose, and if she hadn't scurried under the treacherous falling portcullis and into the little cell, she would have been killed for sure."

Catherine! She was really locked in there! For a spinning instant I could not answer. Finally in a voice low and cracked with emotion, I queried, "How long was she there?"

"Longer than you, of course. Since we didn't know where to look at first. But then I remembered her desire to work in the oubliettes. I warned her not to go there alone, for the cells had only just been uncovered, but she was quite"—he looked away—"some called her brazen, but she was intelligent and eager to learn about the place. Anyway, when I found her, she was as unhinged as any woman could be. She even claimed to have seen an apparition, you know, of the priest. A long time in such a place will ignite one's imagination."

The Haunting of Victoria

He apparently believed the portcullis had fallen of its own accord, but I did not. Someone stood at the top and released that spiked gate. Fortunately they had missed both their victims. Both times. And it wasn't hard to guess that Catherine had not been missed the second try. But who would do such a pernicious thing? Unless there was a strain of bad blood that had filtered down, through centuries, from that first dastardly Rothesay to the present one.

I swallowed down the acidic taste of fright. "And you thought I would be attracted to such a place as well as the historian?"

A bleakness suffused his whole being. "Yes, rather," he grumbled.

How could he know me so well? I rattled on.

"I assume you came to see me this afternoon for some reason and, finding me gone, asked Eva where I was. Then knowing you had given me the Tavistock book to arouse my interest, you went looking for me in the dungeons, too, thinking to find me there. Just like . . . the other woman?"

His expression changed slightly. It seemed to say, "Aha, so you have found me out!"

"Miss Durnham"—his voice was moderated between a laugh and a sneer—"do you think I would purposely expose you to some harm? That the book was intended to arouse your interest, as you say, and get you into trouble?"

I felt my lips harden in protest. I wanted to say that I most certainly did, but I couldn't. Not now.

"No, I don't. It seems a coincidence, that's all."

He paused and looked unendurably unhappy.

Without warning, I felt compassion that I'd never expected to feel toward my employer. Why was he so forlorn?

"I have left you"—he cleared his throat—"the hat in your room. I hope you will wear it to the ball."

A surge of blood rushed to my head. That is why he came looking for me! How embarrassed I was, but how unashamedly excited that he had remembered! I picked uneasily at a loose thread on my skirt. Fool, I chided myself, for letting this man charm you with a gift.

"Thank you, but I hope to repay you," I said firmly.

"Why do you resist so hotly, madam?"

Was that a smile he was hiding? He must be laughing at me! I thought, my cheeks reddening.

"I am your employee, and I feel uncomfortable . . . accepting gifts from you."

"It is not meant as something personal, madam. Only as a token of our appreciation." His voice was soft as silk, and I felt more and more ridiculous by the moment.

Thankfully before I could reply, a door slammed above us and the padding of steps came treading down from the interior of the tower. Heavier, uniform steps followed.

"Victoria! You've been ill, you silly child, not so fast!" came an exasperated voice that I recognized at once as belonging to Margaret.

He turned to me quickly. "Ill?"

"Yes, I . . . she was sick after lunch today. She was resting when I left her with Eva. If she had not improved, I was going to call you and her mother, but she seemed—"

Victoria came upon us. Her wild untamed hair billowed around her pale face and dark eyes. Her pinafore was fresh and starched, however, and she had a spring to her step as if she were excited about something.

She brushed my hand quickly and signaled for both of us to follow.

Margaret's form materialized in the hallway, and I blinked at her image. She was draped in a silky material soft as butter, her hair sparkling with tiny studs of yellow, her eyes reflecting the warm glow of the wall sconces, and I thought how lovely she looked for a woman who had been so long abed!

She said, "Miss Durnham, thank God! I've missed you. Are you all right?"

"Yes, I think so." But my voice was weak.

She scrutinized me a moment and turned to the marquess. "Darling, Victoria's got something to show you. Her painting is finished. I haven't seen it yet, but I can tell she's elated about it. She is particularly set"—her glowing eyes fastened on me—"on having you see it, too, Miss Durnham."

The Haunting of Victoria

The marquess's face creased into a smile. "Let's have a look, then, at this new masterpiece!" he said, and winked at Margaret.

Letting uncle and niece gallop ahead of me, I turned to Margaret, inquiring about the girl's health.

She regarded me stiffly for a moment and said with unexpected harshness, "What did you do? Get lost in the dungeons? Eva told me that Victoria was sick, and after seeing my daughter, I knocked on your door to give you the new hat that James purchased for you. I was astonished to find you gone, especially with my daughter sick. Oh, I hope you don't mind that I left the hat in your rooms?"

"No," I said. "Not at all."

"Then when Eva told me you had taken the afternoon off to tour the castle, I worried about you. There are so many dangerous passages, you know, due to rotting wood and spiders and things! Since James was out all day, I couldn't calm myself until you were safely restored in your rooms. Are you all right, dear?"

A tingling gripped my neck. He had lied about bringing the hat!

"The master never came to Victoria's rooms to ask my whereabouts?" I managed.

Of course he hadn't. He had been surprised that Victoria was ill. How had he known where I was? Unless. Unless . . .

She laid her long fingers on my arm, and for a moment she seemed alarmed, too, but caught herself. "I was with Victoria and Eva for several hours, and he did not come in."

As I followed her sweeping figure up the winding stairs, she changed the subject. "Victoria is much better now. Eva gave her the water, and her color has returned."

"I'm sure she'll be fine," I reassured hollowly.

The mood that settled upon me was chilling, and I could not be released. But nothing prepared me for the grave-faced, silent marquess that I saw when we entered the schoolroom. Victoria was biting nervously on her thumbnail, her eyes as transparent as glass.

Both stared at the canvas.

"Oh! Is something wrong? Let me see!" Margaret called, and went to them.

The look that settled upon her face was nothing less than sheer horror. What could it be? Filled with bewilderment, I went to view the painting myself.

It took a moment to register that though I looked at a woman in a Restoration-era gown, the famous jewels at her ruff-trimmed neck, it was not the head of the beautiful Margaret sitting on those shoulders. Staring at me from the soft-edged world of the watercolor was my sister, Catherine!

Chapter Eight

DID YOU KNOW the lady in the painting? Victoria slid her query onto my dressing table.

I stopped pulling my hair into a braid and stared at the note. Then at the girl. What could I say?

Feeling my gaze upon her, Victoria sat irresolutely on the tufted chair next to my dressing table, looking away from me.

Overcoming my amazement and even a little fright, I held up my answer: *She seemed familiar, that's all.*

She didn't answer, and miraculously seemed to accept what I had told her. She seated herself and watched me finish my toilette with an anticipation that grew with each moment.

How dangerously close I had been to revealing my secret that day! The shock on my face must have betrayed me, even though I had made a fumbling attempt to ask who the lady could be.

Three days had passed since Victoria's shocking painting had been unveiled. Like a detective absorbed in piecing together clues, I had been almost unaware of the brisk preparations for the Rothesays' engagement ball that were happening all about me.

As the momentous evening approached, potted palms and tubs of exotic blooms from the castle's greenhouse filled the ballroom. The rugs were rolled up and the floor waxed for dancing. The expansive stone balcony off the ballroom was set up with tables and chairs, and the walls vibrated to the notes of minuets and waltzes.

Meanwhile Victoria was already absorbed in a new study, allowing me time to observe—as if through a mist—the quiet buzz of excitement that filled the air. The pleasant interlude was a welcome intrusion into my life, so focused on the search for my sister.

Now this evening, in only a few minutes, the grand engagement ball would take place.

I glanced at the girl before me. Eva had helped Victoria dress earlier. Her hair was curled in loose rolls, ornamented with little diamond stars, and in her grown-up silk petticoats and soft wisteria-colored gown, she was transformed into a lovely young woman.

I finished my braid and twisted it at the nape of my neck, arranging soft curls around my forehead. I stepped out of my cotton robe and reached for the gown I had so laboriously reworked. It was certainly not the height of style, but it was more elegant than it had been before. The fitted bodice was cut with a low, pointed neckline and the aqua chiffon material was wrapped around with a knotted bow at the shoulders. A delicate ruffled flounce had been added to the waistline. The skirts were straight, and the underskirt opened nicely to reveal the jutting bustle.

I winked at Victoria, who gaped at me with admiration. I picked up the brown hatbox tied with a strung and opened it, lifting out the feathered toque. The marquess's gift—that Margaret had delivered. A rush of horror went through me, but I hid my reaction for Victoria's sake.

Setting the hat on the back of my head and pinning it in place, I surveyed my image in the mirror. How it accented the dress and made my eyes look larger! I fastened simple drop pearls on my ears and added a plain pearl choker around my neck—gifts from my beau, Thomas, before his death. How ironic that I wore gifts from two men tonight. Two men that I should never be allowed to love.

Victoria was at my side, writing.

You look so beautiful, as if you were a different lady. I mean, you're always pretty, but tonight you will be the prettiest lady at the ball!

I thanked her very much for the fine compliment.

Suddenly I was wistful and a little eager as I strained forward to hear the distant chords of music. What a shame that I had no escort to take me down the grand staircase while I wore my finest of feathers.

I turned a pensive smile upon Victoria.

My mantel clock struck eight as we held hands and left my rooms. None of the guests would see these private rooms in our tower, but nonetheless the gas jets on the wall were turned high. Our skirts rustled along the newly shined floors and the fragrance of flowers hung on the air.

We were rounding the corner of the entrance hall, now filling with guests, when Victoria gripped my arm and gestured to her bodice. Her hands made a "U" motion; it seemed she had forgotten a necklace or article of jewelry.

"I will wait," I mouthed silently, and she scampered up the back stairway we had just come down.

From my vantage point I took a long look at the gallery and the open doorways leading into the East Ballroom. The paneled rosewood walls, milk-glass lamps, Charles II oak armchairs under gilded ceiling and chandeliers were all a pale backdrop to the lovely creatures gowned in rich fabrics, men on their arms, entering the light-filled ballroom.

As I stood gazing admiringly I heard voices behind me. Instinctively I turned to greet the guests, but realized that the voices were coming from the stairs. Their owners were still hidden from view.

"James, she is not working out! I've told you, she's a disappointment. Look what she's got Victoria painting. That's *no* help to my poor girl at all!"

"It's progress, isn't it? Anyway, I've told you that I want to keep Miss Durnham on as Victoria's teacher. I know she can help the girl. And that is my last word!" came James Rothesay's unmistakably curt tone of voice.

"Don't be absurd!"

"I'm not being absurd, madam. Victoria was very attached to Miss Ryce, and when she disappeared . . . well, I think my niece knows something about her disappearance, that's all. Something no one else knows."

Margaret's voice was hard, full of explosive anger. "How could my child know anything? As for attachment," she ground out, "*you* are the only one who was attached to that historian. Putting on all your fancy airs, your gallantry, and underneath you're really a—"

"Will you lower your voice!" he admonished her sharply.

Their steps were close to me, and I whirled into a recess in the wall, which hid me from their view as they came from the stairs out into the hall.

I dared not look, but from the corner of my eye saw his hand fly to her arm and hold her there. I saw a flash of glittering gown as she shrank away from him.

"You will stop acting like the spoiled beauty that you are for one evening and try to enjoy yourself! After all, this damnable party is for you," he spat derisively.

"Oooh, you are so maddeningly arrogant! Not like your brother at all. If only he were alive, he'd get his revenge on you!"

There was a pause. "Perhaps he is getting his revenge, my lovely lady."

"You bastard," she retorted with equal venom, but their tones hastily changed as they began greeting guests.

"Ah, the Rogerses are here!" They moved away from their place in the hall.

The words they spoke echoed in my ears for a hammering instant. The enigmatic marquess was making an impression on me I didn't like. Had he been so fond of Catherine? There was an edge to all this that sounded unmistakably evil.

With unsteadiness that threatened to shake my fragile control, I emerged from the wall, smoothing my skirt and brushing at my hair. A manservant passed quickly by and winked at me!

I was so taken by surprise that I did not stop to think what an amusing picture I must have made. The plain teacher, so enthralled by the handsome marquess, has been reduced to

The Haunting of Victoria 97

snatching bits of private conversation by eavesdropping!

I laughed to myself just as Victoria flew around the corner. Curls flying, eyes bright, and wearing... the lovely pearl necklace her uncle had purchased for her as a special gift for the ball. She handed me the pad with a message scrawled across it.

Remember, you said you would teach me to waltz tonight and let me sip my first champagne!

I assured her that I had, indeed, promised, and once again we clasped hands and walked toward the music and laughter.

We were stopped by the shifting mass of people, and glancing at the main entrance to the ballroom, I realized that the master and mistress had just begun receiving their guests.

Finding an open door closer to us where a bank of white flowers stood, I squeezed Victoria's hand and we followed in the wake of several young women. Gliding inconspicuously into the ballroom, we found a corner close to the French doors where we could watch, unnoticed.

Victoria's eyes were huge and brilliant as she observed the swirl of dancers. Step, two, three. The aristocrats moved as if grace had been bred into them for centuries; the women were graceful as swans, the men pleasantly polite. The chandeliers spilled light like a thousand diamonds onto them, caressing them, making them seem unattainable, belonging to the romantic world of Vermeer or Rembrandt.

And like the artists' world, everything was perfect: huge windows and doors that opened onto the lowering night, the triumphant sound of the violins, silk couches against muraled walls, trays of shrimp and artichokes and pastry with creamed crabmeat, champagne.

A longing rose within me. To dance on that dusted floor to the rhythm of the tender music, to feel my partner's arm pressed against my back...

Victoria and I watched from our private corner for some time before the marquess and Margaret made their entrance. She was dressed magnificently, as always, in deep emerald with diamonds at her ears and neck. Her gown glittered as if a thousand sparkling beads covered it. He was diabolically handsome, in black formal attire, stiff shirt, hair brushed dramatically away from his forehead, teeth flashing in a quick smile.

He was listening to something she said, leaning close, yet distracted, somehow annoyed. Did the lingering effects of their argument make him tense?

I didn't realize that I trembled until the music stopped and people drifted to the sides of the ballroom.

Victoria tugged at my arm, and I followed. She pulled me through the French doors out into the mild evening, where the sky was a velvet canvas dotted with silver, and where a full moon like a yellow wax ball hung on the horizon. Here, too, couples talked and laughed. I heard the sea below and inhaled the scent of the potted roses and azaleas bordering the terrace. Victoria must have felt the vibrations of the music, for she turned to me with her notebook in hand.

May I have this dance, madam? Victoria wrote teasingly.

I answered that, yes, indeed, it was a fine evening to waltz.

The music started again, and though it seemed a long way off, its clear sound obliterated conversation and the murmur of water. We took to the floor with the other glittering guests. I spoke aloud while gesturing to make sure that I was giving proper instruction.

"Now put your hand here on my shoulder, like so. Yes, that's right!"

"And the other hand, here, around my waist, now ... follow my feet if you can see them."

She smiled, and laughing, I hiked up my hem a little as we moved clumsily at the edge of the patio.

"Ah, yes!" I sighed as the tempo picked up, and we tried to move a little faster, but our skirts kept brushing the flowers and she kept stumbling over my feet.

Finally collapsing in a spasm of laughter as the music ended, she and I hugged each other, and I wrote that the next dance would be easier.

A manservant with a silver tray offered us champagne.

"Yes, thank you," I said, taking two glasses. "One for you, Victoria," I said, and we clinked our glasses together.

She gasped a little at first, then drank more greedily as the taste appealed to her. I drank mine, too, letting its intoxicating warmth steal through me.

A hush fell on the ballroom as a new dance was played. A sweet, sad slow song.

Perhaps we can try this one without falling down! I wrote.

We set our glasses on an empty tray at the edge of the loggia and began to sway to the music.

For a moment I was lost in the delightful melody, before looking up and seeing the marquess standing alone in the doorway watching us. His face was in shadow, but I recognized his tall, formidable figure.

I watched him in open fascination as he came toward us with fluid, easy strides, pausing a few steps from us.

Surely the dizzying champagne, the lovely music had affected me, for it was hard to believe that his gaze darkened so dangerously as he looked at me.

I stopped, thankful that the darkness hid my blush. Victoria looked up and was surprised by her uncle's sudden kiss on her cheek. She returned his affection with a squeeze around his neck, and as if responding to some signal, she slowly moved away from us.

"May I?" he asked, taking my trembling hand in his.

"Yes," I whispered.

We said nothing as he drew me slowly, possessively close, his hand tantalizingly firm around my waist. How light I felt, as if I could fly away on the breeze, how his steps matched mine with precision, how easily my head would fit at the hollow of his neck if I should place it there.

Recklessly we whirled to the poignant strains of the song. The music went on, and while it played I became lost to the world, conscious only of him, conscious that my body was reacting of its own accord; I was held by his seductive power, totally his for the moment.

We danced at the edge of the loggia, where the moonlight caught us and, far below, the ocean surged. Neither of us spoke. The spell held.

The music ended, and he released me. But we stood and gazed at each other. His mercurial black eyes studied my face, feature by feature. My heart was pounding, my breath came in short, raspy starts, and an all-consuming weakness crept over me, so encompassing that my eyelids felt heavy.

"You never told me," he said deeply, "that you danced so well."

Victoria ran up to us and thrust a paper into my hand.
Madam, you are blushing!

"Am I?" I turned to her and placed a hand on my cheek.

I could not look at the marquess; I was too embarrassed. For suddenly I was afraid—not of dark dungeons equipped with torture chambers or of ghosts or not finding my sister—I was frightened of myself. The dance should never have happened.

"Thank you," I said uncertainly to him while I grabbed Victoria's hand. "We'll be going back to her rooms now, since it is late. Good night."

"But it is early," he said.

I did not answer.

After a moment he added, "I'll have Eva bring up a tray for you."

Remembering my rumbling stomach, and that neither Victoria nor I had eaten dinner because of our excitement, I thanked him again.

I gave him a quick glance before moving away and saw that he was looking toward the ballroom with a dark scowl. As I gathered my skirts and raised my eyes I saw in utter dismay the figure his frown was focused on. Margaret stood in the doorway, her gown glowing as if lit of its own accord, her head cocked to one side, her lace fan moving.

Without warning, the master was at my side, moving ahead of me, toward her. Certainly he would tell her that our dance meant nothing! That, indeed, it was only a spin

The Haunting of Victoria

around the terrace to make the teacher feel more at home . . . that no harm was intended.

He reached Margaret, touching her elbow lightly as they glided away. She seemed to make no fuss, and swift as lightning, they were lost in the crowd.

Victoria and I were soon in her rooms again, but before I could sit down, she was writing a question for me.

Do you like my uncle? He really is quite nice when he is not angry.

Telling myself I had nothing to apologize for, I answered honestly. *Yes, he is very nice, but you mustn't think he is always angry. Perhaps he has good reasons for it. Anyway, tonight he showed me a courtesy by dancing with me.*

Victoria's smile was pleased, conspiratorial. She was a young lady who knew much more than I gave her credit for.

I quickly changed the subject. *Don't your uncle and mother make a good pair? Did you see how pretty she looked tonight in her emerald gown? And I'm sure she saw how stunning you looked tonight, too.*

She sighed and glanced away distractedly. I thought, with a terrible stillness of my heart, how little Margaret had noticed Victoria—if she had noticed her at all. How dreary to be the daughter of a woman who held court wherever she went, who was breathtaking in her beauty.

To my surprise the girl picked up the pencil again and started writing. *My mother is very pretty, but I sometimes wonder how much she loves me. I know she does, but she is so fond of Uncle James that she forgets me. Occasionally I wonder if she loved my own papa as much as Uncle James.*

There was no answer for this, but I assured her that most probably Victoria's mother loved her father very much. I remembered on a shivering breath how Margaret had accused Rothesay of not being like his brother at all. Yes, her tone was accusatory. What had Victoria's real father been like? Probably not angry or haughty or intimidating.

Remember, Victoria, I was raised by only one parent, too, and there were times when Father was so absorbed in his work that he seemed oblivious to me. But I always knew he loved me. Just as I know your mother loves you. Very much.

Yes, I suppose Mother loves me, she answered, but her face was grim.

She was pensive. Suddenly her expression changed, and she turned to me with a shy smile. Impulsively she reached up and hugged me 'round the neck. Her action was so innocent and honest, I felt the sting of tears behind my eyes.

I'm sorry I've made your stay here so difficult, she wrote, and paused to look up at me. *I guess I do need a friend, after all.*

I thanked her profusely, for this was what I had waited to hear from her.

She was writing another message. *I'd like to go to bed now, but I was wondering if you could stay the night again? I think I'd sleep better if you were here. I never get ill in the mornings if I rest well. It's only when I sleep restlessly and have nightmares that I become sick. Mother said it's owing to bad nerves and overstimulation.*

I assured her that yes, it would be wonderful to spend the night, but asked her if she cared to wait up until Eva brought the tray of food that the marquess had promised?

She would, indeed. She smiled drowsily, lying wearily on the settee. I turned low the wick on the beside lamp, sending the room in deep shadow, except for the bright hearth.

The night was too young and alive with energy to be ignored. I was restless and went to the shutters and opened them. The cool air poured over my shoulders, the silvery strains of music filtered in, the moonlight was high and slanting. Below me I visualized the pretty couples swirling to the music. James and Margaret among them . . .

There was a determined knock at the door that shook me out of my reverie. I glanced at Victoria, who sat up suddenly, looking very frail in the half-light.

The door opened slowly and the marquess entered with a bottle of wine in his hand. He was followed by a manservant carrying a silver tray laden with food.

"Over there on the table," the marquess ordered. The waiter laid down the tray, spreading Victoria's little table with cutlery and linen for two.

"Good Lord, how can you see in here? Let's put some light on the subject." He strode over to the lamp and lit it with a long taper he fetched from the mantel. The room was bathed in light.

I stared, feeling a rush of excitement at his unexpected entrance. Victoria watched him eagerly, and I could see that she was becoming animated.

"Really, this is unnecessary," I heard myself saying. "I thought Eva would bring us a light snack; you've no need to—"

"I'm perfectly aware of what I am doing, Miss Durnham. I enjoyed selecting the items on the tray for you and Victoria, and I hope you enjoy eating them. Oh, and this wine is for you."

He handed me a black-tipped bottle with a dusty label. "From our cellars. It's a good vintage. I think you'll enjoy it."

I turned the bottle in my hands. "Thank you for this lovely surprise."

He reached over and lifted the bottle from me. For a moment his hand brushed mine and a surge of delight swept through me.

"If you'll allow me, Miss Durnham, to open it for you. I'd recommend letting it breathe for a few minutes before drinking. It has quite a good earthy taste, which is very pleasant."

I smiled and said, "I'm sure it will be delicious."

He smoothly pulled out the cork as if he had done so many times before. Victoria's face was bursting with such joy that it broke my heart to see how little was needed to make her happy.

He set the bottle gently on the silver tray, wiping the lip with a napkin. He sniffed the cork and laid it down, too. He shot me a sidelong glance.

"I haven't told you how that lovely toque suits you."

Reflex made me touch it distractedly.

"Your gown is pretty, too. I'm glad to see that the hat matches so perfectly. Mercifully you didn't let pride stand in the way of your wearing it tonight."

That maddening blush crept up my cheeks. I was at a horrible disadvantage because, it seemed, he sensed feelings in me that I tried so hard to disguise! Pride, indeed! What a stupid fool to wear my emotions on my sleeve!

"It was kind of you to notice," I answered.

"Forgive my disagreement, but kind is definitely the wrong word," he said.

"Polite then, you are polite to notice."

To my intense chargin he threw back his head and laughed. In a swift movement he came closer and put his hand on my shoulder.

"Miss Durnham," he said with astonishing tenderness. "I only wanted to please you with my gift of the hat. But it seems you are trying to spurn my hospitality. Is it so difficult to understand why a man notices a pretty young woman like yourself?"

His eyes sparkled mischievously as though he were playing a game. What had Margaret called him earlier? She'd said he put on fancy airs, was gallant, but underneath he was . . . He hadn't let her finish.

"Allow me to disagree with you, sir. I am not spurning your hospitality. It is only—"

I looked away, at a loss for words. I wanted to drop our silly banter, to meet his look openly and honestly with my own. But I was painfully aware that I couldn't.

His face sobered and his hand fell from my shoulder.

"I'm sorry," I said.

"I have always thought that a gift from a man was so— you know, personal."

He remained standing close, and though I was uneasy with his closeness, I felt indescribably happy. His gaze was on me, steady, intense, and in a swift, easy movement he touched the pearls at my neck.

"These are no doubt from a special man in your life?"

I faltered. It would be unendurable to think of Thomas again. Dear, wonderful Thomas who had been a genius in the art world, who had loved me and died so young... leaving me alone.

"Yes, they are from someone who played an important role in my life."

"He is no longer in your life?" He dropped his hand.

"No, he is deceased."

I decided to offer no more information. That Thomas had died in a steamboat explosion a few days before our wedding could matter nothing to the marquess.

"I'm sorry. It is not easy to begin again, is it? To put the past behind you and go forward?"

I studied him. His manner was grave. I believed in that instant he was referring to himself.

"It never is."

"But one must. Life is so short, and to hold on to grief is so... well, pointless somehow. Don't you think?"

I called him to task. "You speak as if you, too, are trying to forget."

"Perhaps in a way I am. Life changes constantly, and what a person had yesterday is many times gone tomorrow."

"You have lost something, then?"

"More to the point, someone."

My head buzzed and my knees were weak. Whom had *he* lost?

He answered my silent query. "I have lost a part of myself. But, then, I suppose we all do, and it is payment for life. As the snake sheds his skin, so must we shed ours, but the new layer is tougher, coarser."

I shivered at his analogy. "Yes, perhaps that is true."

Though his eyes were on me, he didn't see me.

"Would you be insulted if I told you that you remind me of a woman I once knew? I can't put my finger on it. It's the way you turn your head, your American accent, your smile."

My chest felt as if there was no air left to breathe. Of course I knew who he was going to say—my sister. But what else did he want to say about Catherine?

I answered for him. "The American historian that vanished, no doubt? Although I know no reason that we are alike, except that we are both from the same country."

"Yes," he said, "it's uncanny."

I glanced down. He knows! He brought up this topic deliberately. He wants to play on my emotions, taunt me, try to trick me into betraying myself. Suddenly I knew why I interested him so much—he knew more about me than he was letting on!

Victoria rattled a dish on the tray, shooting us an inquisitive look.

I took her cure and made for the silver dishes of delicacies. My hand wavered over the butter-dripping asparagus and the crisp pastries overflowing with creamed crab when he grabbed my wrist.

"Allow me to serve you."

Shocked at his gesture, I relented and drew away, feeling the warmth of his grip long after he had released me.

How much more did he know about me? I wondered as I watched him parcel out the aromatic supper. His hands were deft and sure at his task, and within moments he brought me a beautiful plate with far too much food.

"Thank you for this," I said, and he nodded silently.

He brought Victoria an equally heaping portion, and to my delight I saw that she began eating like any normal, hungry girl.

As he poured the wine for me I thought, Should I play the fool and let him lead me into the darkness into which Catherine vanished? Or would I vanish, too?

"This is for you, Miss Durnham."

I accepted the glass gratefully, but he hovered over me. I inhaled, then drank the ruby liquid. It was smoother than any wine I had ever had, and I was sure it was the oldest. The warmth seeped into my bones like fire.

"It's wonderful." I looked up at him.

He was frowning. "Shall we dispense of the formalities a little? I'd like you to call me James. After all, you are a member of the household now. And if you'd like, I could call you Miss Anne?"

"Not Miss. Just Anne is fine. If that would be appropriate." What was I getting myself into?

The Haunting of Victoria

"Thank you," he said, and his words were soft as a sigh.

"You haven't shown me any of your new paintings since you've arrived here, and I feel that I'm missing something."

I smiled, setting my wine on a table. "You're missing nothing. My paintings so far have been only quick washes, practice runs, you might call them. As the weather turns warmer we'll be setting up our easels outside. The natural light is magnificent. And then when I paint something brilliant, I will let you know!" I said with a laugh.

"You're too modest. I have a feeling that your work is quite good, and I will be honored to see it."

My paintings, since I had been here, were adequate. But I knew I could do better, and I would certainly save my best to show him.

"I will be glad to show you my next painting," I said quietly, then rushed on.

"Victoria is working on something else now, but"—I stammered at my inadvertent mention of Victoria's work—"it will be pleasing, I'm sure. Different from her portrait. Victoria is very talented, as you've told me. She has a gift. And she is surrounded by such an atmospheric setting, there is certainly no lack of subject matter to paint."

His face beamed, and I wondered if he mocked me again. "You are taken with this old castle, aren't you?"

"Who wouldn't be?" But my voice was defensive.

"And you find the people inside it equally fascinating?"

"You have to admit that the people here are far from average; even your ancestors that lived long ago were . . . unusual."

"Yes, unusual."

He looked distracted. "For your own safety, Anne, don't wander about by yourself anymore. That's an order, not a request," he said sternly. "I'm beginning to think there is more truth to the rumor of the dead priest haunting this place than I want to admit."

I gave him a sharp look.

"Well..." He glanced at his niece, who had happily cleaned her plate and was writing him a note. He went to her and read the note in which she explained she had tasted her first champagne tonight, and that she expected to drink it more often!

He laughed and kissed her cheeks. "Sleep well, my angel."

I stood up.

"Though I would rather spend the evening here, I'd better see to my duties downstairs," he said, coming toward me.

"A party is no longer a celebration when it becomes a duty."

"You're so right. Nevertheless..." His voice was low, and he looked at me unguardedly. Then he raised a dancing brow and said good night.

And left us.

I was full of doubts, full of feelings that I did not want to admit. But in spite of my stew of emotions, I knew one thing for certain: Both of us had stepped far beyond propriety's boundaries tonight.

Chapter Nine

IT WASN'T LONG before Victoria undressed and crawled into her bed. I turned the lights low again and pulled the covers close about her head. I went straightaway to my rooms to get my overnight things.

When I returned, I glanced at her curled-up form, her long lashes fanned over her cheeks, her breath soft and even, and knew that she was already sound asleep.

The room was as I had left it. Smoldering logs burned in the now dying fire and a white shaft of moonlight poured through the windows. Victoria lay in its bright, diagonal light, her skin made waxy by the silvery beam.

Reassured that she rested well, I went to the settee and lay down, pulling a quilt over me.

The strains of a Hungarian melody filled the room, and visions of the marquess kept playing in my head. How early it was to go to bed, I thought, and decided to stop fighting the restlessness that plagued me. Sitting up, I determined to fetch my novel and read myself to sleep, when I heard a noise.

It was only a bare whisper of sound—only the most discerning ear could hear it. But I heard it and knew, instinctively, that it wasn't coming from below. It sounded like the squeak of a mouse—or a door hinge. And it was in this room.

Without breathing I lowered myself back down to the couch and lay perfectly still, thankful that I was far enough from the fire to be out of its dying rays.

For a moment there was silence. I heard Victoria's rhythmic breathing and the galloping of my heart in my throat.

I waited, wondering if my imagination had been dizzily overworking.

Then, stealthily, carefully, came the unmistakable padding of feet proceeding from a dark corner of the room. Suddenly, from out of the shadows, a long, black shape stabbed across the patch of moonlight!

I could see that it was a draped in a floor-length cloak with an insidious hood pulled horribly over its head! Was this the ghost of the priest?

A quick terror clutched me, and I wanted to scream, but my mouth was dry as paste. I turned my head a fraction to follow the horrifying silhouette that had materialized from the secret passageway. It headed toward Victoria's bed.

The phantom leaned over Victoria, and I strained to see its face. But the figure was backed by the light, and the face obscured. It reached out to touch the girl, and I stifled the gasp that rose in my throat. It raised its arm up slightly, the full sleeve falling back, and I saw with horror that it wore black gloves! It hovered a trice at Victoria's bedside table.

What would it do to the child? I was poised, with every fiber of my body, to jump out at the intruder the moment it tried to harm Victoria.

Nothing happened.

The demon walked away and went toward the murky alcove filled with stuffed bears. Away from me—and the girl. The hair on my skin bristled, my neck craned around stiffly to get a better view. But the silhouette was lost in darkness.

There was only menacing silence, and I waited, praying that it wouldn't lunge at me.

What was the phantom doing there in the corner? Was it watching me? Did it know I was here? Then came a muffled, tearing sound, and I thought I would faint from fear.

The stuffed bears! It must be stabbing them with a knife. The insanity behind such a cruel act was more frightening than my lying there, helpless.

The Haunting of Victoria 111

Abruptly the destructive ripping sounds halted. I was filled with dread.

What now? Was the sword, which I imagined swinging in a gleaming hilt, sheathed again? Or was it out, ready and aimed at its next victim?

The tinkling of a piano filled the air, and with a new rush of fear, I heard the soft pad of steps coming back across the room. The figure passed through the sheen of moonlight, its treacherous form pausing a moment, before moving on again into shadow. There was a low thump as the door in the wall closed. It was gone!

A prickly sensation of relief washed over me, but I didn't dare move, didn't dare breathe until I was perfectly sure. . . .

An eternity passed. I slowly, noiselessly, sat up and pulled back the cover. My feet met the cold floor and I stood. Carefully, carefully, making sure my treads were light as feathers, I went to the wooden door leading to the secret passageway. For a frozen moment I stood there, my hand slipping on the knob.

There was no way of locking it on the inside, so with painstaking effort I half carried, half pulled a ponderous oak chair and set it against the door. Then I hurried to Victoria's bedside.

She was breathing normally; she hadn't even changed position since she had fallen asleep. I held my chest, my hands trembling like leaves. She was unhurt!

Inadvertently leaning back too suddenly against her bedside table, I knocked over her hot chocolate, but caught it before it spilled. A thought whirred in my head. It was farfetched, but still . . .

I took the drink and smelled it. There was a sharp, musky aroma. Alarmed, I glanced nervously around me and, clutching the cup in my hand, made for the settee and placed the full cup under it. I would keep it for now.

I was at Victoria's bedside again, picking up her ivory Pierpoint lamp, turning up the gas. Bathed in its glow, I moved falteringly across the room—toward the shadowy corner where the apparition had been.

Slumped against each other on a wooden shelf were the group of floppy little bears. Their button eyes stared quizzically at me.

They looked intact. Except for a fuzzy brown one that was sprawled facedown away from the others. I picked it up and stuffing fell out in my hands.

"Oh!" I gasped.

Its torso and legs and arms had been slit wide open. What was the purpose of this vile act? As I held the unraveling bear against my chest and stepped quietly back to my bed, I refused to answer my question.

I crawled under the covers and the bear came with me.

The angle of the moonlight had changed, and now my settee was spotlighted in the slanting rays. I lay awake, thinking about the demon and his awful errand, until the moon had moved from its position in the sky, until an inky blackness covered me, until scarlet streaks colored the eastern horizon. Then my shocking answer surfaced. For an inexplicable reason the ghost priest thought the Rothesay jewels were hidden in this room! I was certain it had searched for them inside the bear.

Finally I fell asleep.

The next morning when Victoria had awakened and left for the schoolroom, I did not linger in bed. Arising immediately, I took the stuffed bear and cold cup of cocoa and went to my own rooms. Jobelle brought my tray of tea and pastry, and I told her it was important that I have an interview with the mistress. As soon as possible.

After a hot bath, I dressed in a plain blue frock with a high collar and pulled my hair to the top of my head, fastening indigo clips on each side. It was important that my look match my grave manner.

Margaret would see me right away. She had had a bad night and was eating breakfast in her rooms, and if it was not inconvenient, I could see her there.

I grabbed the cup of cold chocolate, and Jobelle led me through a labyrinth of winding halls and stairs that led to the North Range of the castle. We entered Margaret's suite of rooms, and I was led into the boudoir that adjoined her bedroom. I felt embarrassed at being in the intimate room and wondered how often the marquess was here with her.

My quick survey of the room gave me a distinct impression: it was romantic, languid, salacious. Its decor was vaguely Eastern, all black-and-gold opulence. But the colors were heavy and oppressive.

Though sunlight pressed in at the windows, heavy brocade drapes closed it out. Stone arches, bordering the sleeping alcove, were studded with bright bits of glass that glowed like myriad insect eyes. Smoke-glass lamps in curving, sensual shapes lent a soft glow to the room. It was evident that this gentle illumination enhanced the loveliness of the reclining woman in her bed.

Margaret was propped against lacy pillows, her face drawn, her eyes huge against the pallor of her skin, and her hair fell in a cascading mane about her shoulders. She sipped from a china cup and picked delicately from a bowl of grapes before inviting me to draw a chair close to her bed.

I did so, catching sight of myself in the tall mirror over her dressing table. My reflection was startling. My skin had a faint color to it against the deep blue dress, my hair was deep, almost black, and my eyes were luminous. I was intent on a mission.

"Lady Rothesay," I began dubiously. "I fear your daughter is in grave danger."

Instead of surprise or alarm, which I expected from her, she merely reclined her head and looked at me warily. Her somnolence was disturbing, and I wondered, again, if she was under the influence of a drug.

"In what way?" she rasped, setting her tea on her lap tray.

"If you'll allow me to speak plainly?"

"What other way is there?" she asked.

Ignoring her bluntness, I explained what had happened last night. That as soon as Victoria was in bed, the menacing specter of a priest came into her room, touched her face, and ripped open one of her stuffed bears in search of something.

"And I fear that when Victoria becomes ill, it is not because of nerves. Here, look at her cocoa from last night."

I handed Margaret the cup of chocolate for her inspection. It didn't take a medical expert to detect the tarry black substance around the rim. But I carefully avoided mention of what I feared the most.

She sloshed the chocolate around the cup and dipped a long finger into the substance. Hesitantly she tasted it with her tongue and made a bitter grimace. She held the cup possessively.

"Well, what do you think it is?" she asked, her face suddenly tight with concern.

"I am no professional in the field of pharmacology, nor am I trained in the medical arts."

"Yes?" she prodded.

"I think it could contain either opium or morphine," I said, meeting her gaze.

She lowered the cocoa to the tray. I noticed how her hand trembled.

"I will keep this until I can see my doctor. He will test it for us," she said unevenly.

Then she raised her arm to her forehead as if she were in a swoon. Her eyes glazed for a moment, her lids drooped. She released a thready breath.

"Madam, are you all right?" I stood and reached out to her.

"Yes," she answered tremulously. "I . . . it's that I didn't expect to hear this."

"I'm sorry to have to give you such disturbing news. Thankfully I spent the night with Victoria and kept the chocolate away. No harm has come to her yet, but it may come, soon, Lady Rothesay. Soon."

I folded my suddenly cold hands together in a firm clasp.

"I can't say why this should be, but I believe that someone thinks Victoria is hiding something in her rooms. I was thinking . . . Lady Rothesay, do you believe that the Rothesay jewels are still on the premises? The ones that were hidden during the Inquisition?"

She pulled at her hair girlishly, rolling it in a ponytail, and refused to meet my look.

"Why do you ask that?" she said finally.

"Because I think"—I sat down slowly—"that someone is wearing the costume of the rumored ghost priest only in order to search Victoria's rooms. To look for the jewels. And for some incomprehensible reason, this person believes the jewels are in Victoria's possession. I am beginning to think that Victoria knows where they are, too, and if she regains her, well, her health, she may discover them. But it's my opinion that someone is determined to get there first."

The last shred of Margaret's detached manner gave way, and she covered her face with her hands. Her grief moved me to pity, and I sat uncomfortably still while she cried in great gulping sobs.

After a little while she lowered her hands and pulled a delicate handkerchief from her robe's sleeve. She wiped her eyes and blew her nose.

"I'm sorry," I said. "Let me help in any way I can."

She didn't hear me. "It's... it's those blasted gems! I don't know why James bothers." She looked at me, her eyes moist and red.

"He's digging for them, uncovering every godforsaken remnant in this cursed area to get at them. I don't know why he is so insistent."

I couldn't let her see my discomposure. I queried as calmly as I could, "You mean, the jewels really are hidden here somewhere?"

"Oh, that's what everyone claims." She dabbed at her eyes again. "Miss Durnham, the Rothesay family is rapidly running out of money! Our fortune is dwindling! It is James's last prayer, last hope, to hold on to these lands. And he can't do so without a lot of money. Right now the National Trust is supporting our work; in return we let the tourists come through, we give up our privacy in order to live here. Oh, you don't know what I suffer!"

She grasped at her handkerchief and tried to dab away a new onslaught of tears.

"It must be very uncomfortable for you," I said.

"It's worse than that. No one knows. No one knows how dismal it is to live in a castle, to spend every pound for keeping this place intact, for restorations. I smile, I charm, I wear my loveliest gowns, for our guests from the Tourist Board and the County Council, and for what?" She groaned. "So that tomorrow it will all be taken away?

"And now this! Now my own flesh and blood at the mercy of some maniac who believes they will find our only treasure left to us! It isn't fair! 'S not fair!"

I handed her a clean handkerchief of my own. "You're right. It is unfair, but you must not forget how important Victoria is. And how threatened her life is right now. Do what you must to prevent the thief from taking the jewels, but keep in mind that Victoria is your real treasure! She is the one who must be saved at all costs."

Her face cleared a little, and she sighed. "You're right, of course. It's just that I have been so involved in all these worries, it's hard to see how my own daughter suffers."

"Or may suffer," I said gently.

Her eyelashes fluttered for an instant as though this thought was unbearable. She pushed away her tray of food and gave me her full attention. A shiver ran through her as she looked at me.

"There is something . . ." she began, splaying her delicate fingers against the silk counterpane. "And now that you know what our situation is, I hope you do not take it badly, or believe that we were unhappy with you."

It didn't take much detective work to guess what she would say, but I kept a closed mouth and waited for her to continue. I could not let her see my discouragement, so I squared my shoulders and prepared myself for her next statement.

"James and I have discussed it, and, oh, please do not take this the wrong way"—she beamed a smile and was suddenly younger and prettier—"but we cannot afford to keep you, Miss Durnham. In spite of all the help you have been to us—and to Victoria."

Though she smiled apologetically, her rigid tone and unwavering gaze told me it was pointless to try to change her mind. I knew I must accept her verdict, for whether I wanted to admit it or not, she had undoubtedly seen the marquess and me together last night. It would benefit me to admit defeat, and keep my dignity.

I had been steeling myself for this all along, but nothing prepared me for the feeling that I had somehow failed. And beyond that, I was ashamed. Ashamed because I would miss my employer.

I quickly reprimanded myself for such foolish regrets. The girl's future was what really mattered now.

"And Victoria?"

Her smile dimmed, and she looked away. "She has done so well under your tutorship that I believe she will continue to paint on her own now. It seems to me that she is on her way to recovery."

"If you truly believe this, Lady Rothesay, then do not shirk your duty to her. I implore you as one woman to another, take time with your daughter; she needs you. I know she will recover, but you are the only sun she can warm to."

Suddenly Margaret's face was animated by an emotion I did not like. Her amber eyes turned cold, and she seemed to emanate disdain. I had said more than she wanted to hear.

"You've been here almost a month, Miss Durnham?"

"Yes, that is correct."

"Then I hope you do not feel that we are 'shirking our duty' to you by letting you go at this time?"

Her note of sarcasm made me draw back. "Lady Rothesay, I did not mean to offend. I am only thinking of your child and what is best for her."

"I know that, too," she said distractedly. "It's just that I am trying to do the best I can with a very difficult child."

I nodded.

"If only we could keep you . . . but then, we have lost so many good things in this unfortunate affair of ours."

"There is no need to excuse what must be done," I said carefully.

"I will see to it that James pays you fully what you are owed, and that the proper testimonials are drawn up in order for you to procure another position."

Abruptly she yawned and patted her mouth. "Pardon me, the party last night and all . . ."

Lethargy had fallen upon her again, and I knew the interview had come reeling to a halt. I stood, saying, "I will send Gavin for a timetable of the trains, and I will begin packing immediately. I will leave as soon as possible."

Though I wanted to walk away and never lay eyes on Margaret again, I hesitated with one last question. "Lady Rothesay, I'd like to ask your permission to move Victoria's teddy bears into my quarters—permanently. I've no doubt that the dastardly thief will return, and since I will no longer be living there, no harm could come to anyone."

"No," she said listlessly. "Don't put your life in peril. Not even for one last night. That is certainly not necessary. Bring them to my rooms right away."

She closed her eyes, and to my surprise I saw a glimmering teardrop on her lash. She blinked and looked away. The meeting had taken its toll on her, and I said good-bye and soberly walked away.

In a few moments I was back in Victoria's rooms, digging through her menagerie of floppy brown bears. I knew the girl was absorbed in a painting in the schoolroom, and hoped she would not come upon me.

I would have to think of a reasonable explanation for removing her animals, I thought. And I gathered them awkwardly in my arms and made for my own suite of rooms.

In my bedroom, I laid the bears next to each other on my four-poster and regarded them. I had little time left here, and this was my last chance to discover what, if anything, was hidden inside these stuffed toys.

I examined the creatures before me. Was the priest really searching for jewels, and if so, what reason did he have to believe they were concealed in such a strange place?

One bear was made of stiff padding and its four feet were rigid; the other five were soft and limp, made of worn plush fabric. One wore a little jacket and cap. Surely I could feel the hardness of stones within these fuzzy creatures if, indeed, any were there.

I took the first one in my hand, examining it, then squeezing it firmly. I probed with my fingers, pushing in on its abdomen, its legs, arms, and head. There was no resistance to my touch. I picked up the second, third, and so on, until I had poked at all the soft ones. It seemed useless, and with discouragement, I picked up the last one, which was hard and unyielding to the touch.

It felt as if it had been lacquered. It wore an ill-fitting jacket, which I removed, turning it over. To my amazement there was a narrow line of black thread zigzagging down its stomach. I pushed at the incision, but it was glazed over with a wax coating.

It took no time to cut through the wax and thread and pry open the inflexible bear with a yank. No sparkling jewel fell onto the floor as I had expected, but out came a small, square book!

In wonder, I picked it up. It was bound in soft purple leather, pink ribbon lacing its spine. I turned to the first page and staggered back. It had belonged to Catherine! The title page read: *My personal account as historian to the Marquess of Wessex; Tavistock Castle, Dover, England.*

It was signed in Catherine's long, looping hand and appeared to be a diary of sorts, detailing the course of her stay here. I scanned to the first page. It was not easy to decipher her scrawled words, but I studied hard. It began:

September 7, 1888: My arrival at last! It's a rainy, cool evening, and I am too tired to let the atmosphere of this fusty old place sink in, yet. Tomorrow I can better tell what I am in for. I have been told by the rather brusque mistress that the esteemed "Marquess" will lead me on a tour of the castle itself and the grounds. He has ambitious plans for renovations and preservation.

Meanwhile, I am warmly housed in a wattle-and-daub weaver's cottage attached in a corner of the bailey wall. I can look out my window and view the looming keep in the distant fog. Oh, what a setting! Tonight, as I sit by my bright fire, I am filled with eager anticipation at what tomorrow will bring.

The next entry was dated two days later.

September 9: So much has happened in only a short time! Where do I begin? For starters, I am finding the inhabitants of this magnificent place as interesting as the work I have begun. If only I were a writer, I'd use these characters in a story. Victoria, Rothesay's niece, is a spritely young thing, full of curiosity, full of questions. She is so intrigued with my presence that I promised to take her along with me one day while I work. The gatekeeper, Hal Mathews, is an irascible old fellow who watches me with something like suspicion. He does not like my presence here. I think he is afraid that I will unearth a pit full of skeletons buried during the Inquisition!

And the master and mistress: the most beautiful couple I have ever laid eyes on. I have never met a man who I could so convincingly call tall, dark, and handsome! I find that I can't take my eyes off him. No wonder Tavistock is so busy with ladies' tours. They are not here to see ruins of former times, they want a glimpse at the dreamy, aloof marquess! Margaret Rothesay is equally elegant, and it is no wonder they are engaged. Two pretty people such as they are should stay together!

There was a long section describing how Catherine had mapped out the land, discovering from the marquess where the buried medieval walls were located, destroyed timber buildings, the original earthworks. Most of these pages were technical in nature, so I skipped over them. Accompanying her notes were thumbnail sketches showing the original floorplan of the keep and the keep as it is today. I came to an entry written four days after her arrival.

September 11: I am exhausted tonight. I worked with three archaeologists today—brought in from London.

The Haunting of Victoria

They will stay on indefinitely. Lord Rothesay held a meeting to let us know his plans. While he wants to restore Tavistock as much as possible to its original medieval splendor—and, I might add, he has done so with the East and North Ranges—he has reason to believe that a great many treasures were hidden in the castle during the Inquisition. Including a diamond necklace and two bracelets with rubies, emeralds, sapphires! Jewels that were hidden here at least three centuries ago! Who can fathom it?

Rothesay told us about the jewelry because of its extreme value. If they are here to be found, they will certainly be priceless! We were each given a copy of a treatise on Tavistock Castle, which contained all the family's history, and were told that it would benefit us to read it.

September 14: I finally finished reading the treatise. Quite an account, I must say. Mostly facts, but if one reads between the lines, it is a fascinating tale of power, love, and treachery.

The marquess has spent the last two days in London, digging in the archives of a library, and he is ecstatic about a discovery he has made! We will meet with him for lunch tomorrow, and I am eager to hear his news.

September 15: Lunch on the patio in the center of the magnificent, very English garden. It has been an uncommonly clear autumn, and everyone tells me to enjoy the mild weather while it lasts.

Lady Rothesay joined our group today. She is a beautiful woman, but underneath her smooth facade I detect a nervousness, almost a desperation. She loves the marquess very much, and I wonder . . . ? No, it is too fantastic. But sometimes I think she might be *jealous* of his attentions toward me. He only speaks to me about the work we are doing, and I feel that he admires me (yes, in spite of everyone else, who believe I am not to be respected as a historian), but there is absolutely no interest in me otherwise. Still she is unkind to me, and turns away when I am present. I must not let this bother me. It is her loss, if she pretends that I do not exist.

The marquess relayed his news in a rather subdued voice. His enthusiasm from yesterday has dampened considerably, which seems odd. But what he had to say is incredible, and it has made us disbelievers see that the jewels most undoubtedly exist. (I was one of the disbelievers.)

When the original owner of the necklace and bracelets—Margaret Rothesay—was sentenced to death by the church, she was taken to her father's torture chambers in the basement of this castle! There, a priest named Father del Rio (I think the name is correct) was said to have mildly tortured her in an attempt to get her to curse Protestantism and embrace the Catholic faith. She refused, and was locked in one of the wretched oubliettes, where straw covered the floor and there was no heating, nor, in fact, light, and she had only meager rations to eat.

Like previous prisoners, she was hung from iron manacles and endured the excruciating agony for hours at a time. According to the marquess, her chamber was the same one in which Father Gerard was tortured and imprisoned before he tried to dig his way out. It is in this secret tunnel that the marquess believes the jewels are hidden.

Lord Rothesay told us that the facts indicate that Margaret wore the precious jewels during her imprisonment in the oubliette, but when she was taken to London, along with her parents, to be beheaded, the jewelry was missing. Evidently they had been hidden in order that the church would not gain possession of them.

It seems logical that they may have been concealed in the terrible tunnel that leads from the cells to the lighthouse. The fusty, moldering walls of such a crude tunnel will have to be examined inch by inch, and the marquess has warned us it will be a thankless job at best, a dangerous, harrowing one at worst.

The Haunting of Victoria

I felt anguished at the prospect of such an unappealing task. Traveling all the way from Minnesota to dig about in a smelly, old passageway!

When I asked the marquess, "Why don't you just continue with your work of preservation, and along the way search for the gems? There is no proof that the gems absolutely exist," he looked at me so harshly that I wilted before him. Then he answered sternly that he knows, for certain, the jewels are here, and that he will find them!

I am beginning to think that he not only needs the money the jewels will provide him, but that he is desperate for it!

Today, for the first time, I wished I had not accepted this commission.

There was a knock at the door. I threw the diary under the silken coverlet and tossed the bears under my bed. Straightening myself, I called, with what little authority I could muster, to enter.

The door opened and the marquess appeared. He wore a deep blue silk smoking jacket, and the color dramatically accented the dark tones of his skin, and his black hair, which was disheveled. His eyes shone with anger.

"I am sorry to disturb you, but I had to see you straightaway." He pulled the door closed softly behind him.

I smiled tentatively.

"I have just come from Margaret." He scanned the room. "I hope you are not packing?"

"Not yet," I answered.

"Then don't start. You are not to leave. Margaret had no business telling—she is unduly worried about our situation here, and for some absurd reason, she thinks by having one less salary we will be saved!"

"If it's what you and Margaret want, I cannot stand in the way of your decision."

He stared at me. "It's not what I want. Do you think I am so blind that I cannot see how happy Victoria has been these last days? Your help has been more than good for her, you have handed her life back to her."

"It is what you paid me to do."

"Confound it, madam, do not act humble! You have achieved great things here, and I should think you would have put up more fight to stay so you can continue the good work."

I stood my ground. "Lady Rothesay believes it is the only course to take."

He wiped a strong hand across his face and lowered his voice. "Do you want to leave?"

"No," I answered quietly.

"Then the matter is settled. I am the master here, and if you wish to stay, then you will."

He paused and looked down. His face was dark, and he seemed in such despair that I wanted to run to him, place my arms about his shoulders, comfort him. I could do no such thing, of course, and watched him with helpless compassion.

When he looked at me again, his guard was down, and I was able to glimpse his vulnerability.

"Do you know what it is like?" he asked slowly, his words raspy. "To be afraid? Really afraid?"

I answered that yes, I did.

He laid a hand on the doorknob, but kept his gaze on my face. "Of yourself?"

I trembled.

"You look very pretty in the morning light, Anne."

And he was quietly gone, the door shutting behind him.

Chapter Ten

I COULD NOT forget the words the marquess had spoken to me that morning. Or how his face looked when he left me. Still I knew that spending my day in compulsive fascination of him was useless, so I turned my mind to other matters.

Fortunately the day's activities intervened, and Victoria and I were kept busy in the schoolroom, painting. She was still secretive about her new project, and I worried over this. She reassured me, however, that no one would see this painting except me. I wasn't sure if that was good news or bad, but I thanked her for her regard.

A soft rain fell continuously, and one could practically see the grass turn green. The inclement weather made staying indoors bearable, and I started sketching a rather charming portrait of Victoria. My motives were entirely selfish, for I knew if this sketch was good enough, I would show the marquess.

Evening came swiftly upon us, and soon it was Victoria's bedtime. She hadn't missed her bears yet, and when she crawled into bed and noticed that they were missing, I reassured her that one of the undermaids had taken them to be cleaned. It was a weak fabrication, but it seemed logical.

I would stay with her tonight, and planned to do so until the macabre events could be explained. Once Victoria was under the covers, secure with knowing that I would spend the night, I lay down on the settee, exhaustedly. A table lamp pouring light over my shoulders, my muscles braced for disaster, I thought. Surely the ghost priest will not come again. Thankfully my mind turned to other matters, and I did not worry about the apparition for the rest of the night. Nor did he appear.

There was no doubt that my staying here was only a respite given by the master, and that sooner or later Margaret would have her way, and I would be asked to leave. With that in mind, I determined to discover any leads to Catherine's whereabouts that I could.

I glanced at Victoria. She was not stirring; she had fallen asleep already. With my heart beating wildly, I pulled my sister's diary from the bundle of blankets I had brought with me from my rooms. I turned to the page where I'd left off.

> September 21: So here I am, digging like a mole into a subterranean passage that goes on forever! I am disgruntled, dispirited, and tired! And so are the others, but Lord Rothesay drives us on. By the eerie glow of flickering torches we keep searching the damp walls, and though to some it would be the stuff of high drama, I am not excited by it. I have had little time to research—perhaps this is *not* the only place where the jewels might be located—but the marquess grows more intense daily. Convinced that this is absolutely where the gems are hidden, he is like a man possessed.
>
> Meanwhile the renovations on the keep and the grounds have come to a halt. We are focused on our single purpose, and we dare not question it. Sometimes I wonder if we are racing against someone else. If we don't find the jewels, they will. But who could that be? And yet as we learn more about Margaret and her jewels, the more I am absolutely convinced that someone is watching, waiting for me to make a discovery!
>
> On top of this, the archaeologists—all men, of course— do not like having a woman historian around. Though no one actually "says" anything, I am an oddity here where women are regarded merely as decorative figures in the background. I am wondering if I should ask the marquess

to let me out of my contract. There is all of Europe in which to work, and Tavistock is too unsettling.

September 30: We have dug halfway through the tunnel, and still there is no sign that anything is hidden here. Full of despair, I made an appointment with the marquess for tomorrow. I will give him my resignation. And now I fall into bed with the knowledge that I have made the right decision.

October 1: I am at my wit's end. The marquess will not let me go! It's peculiar, but he seems to cherish my work immensely. He says I am valuable to his project, and that I should not despair. We are close to finding something. To give me a respite from the backbreaking work of digging, he has granted me time to study in the library.

What a room! Floor-to-ceiling oak bookshelves, stuffed with leather-bound volumes that date back several centuries!

He showed me a whole section of books that were printed during the first Rothesay's time, and among them was a book of poetry written by Margaret! I scanned through it and was delighted to see how well she wrote. Her language, old-fashioned as it now sounds, is beautiful to read aloud. Like music really.

There were some maps, medical and history books, a volume of Plato, and several books written in Latin. Though I was disappointed not to find any personal papers—a diary or letters from one of the family members—I thrilled at the touch of the ancient leather-bound volumes. Holding them seemed to transmit a misty memory of other hands that had touched them long ago.

No discovery as yet in the tunnel; and though I have been temporarily appeased by being allowed to spend more time in research and less in physical labor, something still makes me uncomfortable. I am a little afraid, and yet of what I don't know! Could my intuition be correct or am I just imagining things?

October 15: Two weeks have passed since my last entry, but I have not had the energy to return to my little book. Perhaps it is because when I retire to my cottage at night, I am so tired I could sleep for days! And lately I have had distressing attacks of the ague. Some evenings I go off to bed in a paroxysm of chills and fever, only to awaken in the mornings feeling fine. I attribute my malady to many things: being overworked, my nervous condition. Mainly I have decided not to let my physical ailments worry me overmuch. Much of it is owing to my mental state, anyway. And there is so much to be accomplished.

A discovery has been made at last! Three quarters of the way into the tunnel one of the archaeologists pulled out a small gold-encrusted trunk from a niche in the wall! Once we extricated it and brushed it delicately off, we opened it. It was empty! I told the others that this is undoubtedly a receptacle for small household valuables and could have, at one time, contained the jewels. In medieval times people stored their goods in trunks such as these. There is no doubt that the jewels—if they were once in there—were removed before the trunk was buried. Now the marquess is really convinced that if we complete our search into the lighthouse, the jewels themselves will appear.

This afternoon, a light was shed on some of my suspicions. Having felt poorly again last night, I took time today to walk by the sea. The day was clear, sunshine, mild breeze, sparkling water. Victoria joined me. She is such a lovely little girl. We talked about art, history, about what life must have been like when this castle was new.

We have become fast friends, she and I, for she is curious about me and my work, and she is terribly lonely, I fear. It is harmless to let her follow me around in my daily routine, so when she is not with her teacher, she has become my constant companion.

As we walked today she told me a startling bit of information. She and a good friend from town play often in

The Haunting of Victoria

the ruins, and when they were last in the old lighthouse, something very terrible happened. She was so agitated that she began to cry, and I had to urge her relentlessly to talk.

It happened like this: It was only three days ago—the evening following the discovery of the trunk—when she and her friend were playing inside the lighthouse. It was a damp, cold day and evening was falling fast, leaving the girls to play in the gloom. Immersed in their game, they were oblivious to the lateness of the hour and had mounted the stone steps rising up to one side of the structure. They were on a small platform, peering out a window, when a dark shadow emerged into the space below them. Instinctively they crouched down so that the apparition would not see them, and when they peered closer, they saw that the figure wore a long black hooded cape! He was dressed in some medieval costume resembling a priest's.

The specter hovered 'round in the lighthouse for only a few minutes before hurrying off in the direction of the gatehouse. Victoria is certain that she and her friend were not seen, but her friend refuses to visit again! Her story seized me with terror, and now I know that my fears were real. Someone is watching, waiting for our discovery. Why else would this disguised person come sniffing around?

October 20: I am still in my cottage this morning. My head hurts madly, and I have the shutters closed against the invading light. My hand trembles as I write, but I must put down on paper what my mind so urgently spurs me to say.

Two days ago, while reading in the library, I decided to search the shelves again. In case I missed something. At the far corner of the top shelf I eyed a small red leather notebook. Mounting the wooden ladder with some trouble, I managed to procure the flimsy book. It was ancient, the crinkly cover almost coming apart in my hands. When I opened it, I was astonished! It was in Margaret's hand,

and was dedicated to her son, Michael. (It was through him that the Rothesay name continued, since his life had been spared.)

I read each page, wondering if mother had told son, in some secret code, where she had hidden the jewels. The book was all poetry again, much of it copied from her other book that I had already read.

I was beginning to give up hope when I turned back to the first poem. It reads:

Welcome to Tavistock Castle!
All ye who enter have a care
No hasp is snap't twixt cell and stair,
And for thy freedom's sake beware
That in the well thou are not trap't

I pondered this for a great while. The well . . . it could make sense. They were usually very deep and the jewels could have been tossed down one. All of a sudden something incredible dawned on me: in the oubliette where Margaret was imprisoned, there are scratchings on the wall. *WE* . . . it says. Though none of us gave it much thought when we first spied the letters there—perhaps a dying prisoner had carved the name of his loved one, a noble sentiment—I know now it spelled only one word. *Well!*

Margaret was telling her son to look in the well for the family's jewels! She had left as many hints as possible without giving away her secret.

I left the library and hurried to find the marquess. I found him in the lovely old church. He was kneeling at the alabaster sarcophagus, and I was sure he was praying.

Cautiously approaching him, I spoke his name, and he started out of his reverie as if a gun had been shot! He glanced up at me as if he didn't know me, his face twisted into a grimace so profoundly sad that it looked as though he had been crying!

The Haunting of Victoria

Distraught at having interrupted his private musings, I apologized for my untimely visit, but he insisted that I stay. He wanted me to sit next to him on one of the oak benches, and politely asked what had brought me in such a heated rush. I showed him Margaret's book. I pointed out the crucial poem and told him my conclusions.

I explained my theory that the well was most probably located in the still-ruined South Range. It followed that the water supply would have been situated there, in the safest corner of the castle—away from the gatehouse. He listened patiently, but I did not hold his attention.

Finally he turned to me. His eyes were dark, glaring, his mouth unforgiving.

"Do you know what I have just found out?" he asked.

I shook my head.

"It is something so dreadful, so dangerous, that I cannot begin to tell you."

"If you have discovered a bit of important evidence that may lead to the prized jewels, then you cannot hold it back, sir!" I prodded him.

His face creased into a maniacal grin, and he turned away from me. "No," he said solemnly. "It is not that."

I sat quietly, wondering what to make of his cryptic comment. He is such an enigma, but every day a new layer of his personality unfolds for me. And I have discovered, with shocking clarity, what a great man he really is! Oddly his dashing good looks keep people at a distance. They act as a deflector in order that he may stay private, and it seems he wants it that way. Yet that has caused him isolation and, I think, great loneliness.

As I sat silently touching the worn leather cover of Margaret's book, a thought pierced my core. With what I had told him the marquess knew enough to find the jewels on his own, and I wondered if I could trust him fully.

Finally I stood, making a polite excuse to get back to work, when he grabbed my hands, asking me to leave the premises as soon as possible! That if I stayed on longer, my life would be endangered!

"You are very distressed, sir. I am quite safe, I assure you!" but when I looked at him, his eyes were grave and unresponsive.

"If you stay, your life cannot be my responsibility. You will remain of your own accord."

I trembled at his brittle tone, but asked myself how I could run panic-stricken from a fear that wasn't even tangible? I gathered my wits and returned abruptly to the subject at hand.

"Thank you for your concern, sir, but I am very eager to go back to the oubliette, knowing what I know now. With your permission, I would like to search it alone. I need to study the walls in case there may be more writing that we have not found yet. After that I would like to begin work on the South Range. I will need all your men—or as many as you can spare me—for it will be, undoubtedly, heavy work. If my calculations are correct, and I will make up several maps in order that others may follow them, I am certain that we will uncover a well."

He watched me bleakly and said without enthusiasm, "You are bright and ambitious. And I am grateful for your tenacity in seeing this thing through. I can only hope that all your plans do not come to naught."

My heart sank. What if he was right? For there was Victoria's story about the priest, there is that ominous feeling I carry with me daily, but surely we had all scared ourselves with too many ghost stories.

It was time to defend my territory. "Sir," I told him with a steady look, "I can't begin to guess what it is that you have just heard. It seems that whatever the ill tidings were, you are convinced that my life is in peril. I am grateful for your concern, but I am not one to turn and run at the slightest noise. You have not given me sufficient reason to go, therefore I will stay and, hopefully, complete my work."

It was a bold statement, and I was glad that he could not see how my heart hammered wildly in my chest!

He watched me intently for a sizzling moment, and his face darkened. Then he told me something strange...

strange and out of character for a man of his good sense.

"It is I," he said quietly. "Go, because I can harm you. And I will if you tempt me."

He looked at me so appraisingly that I felt my cheeks flame. Was he insinuating that he was lustful and was, perhaps, attracted to me? No . . . it could not be, simply could not be. Yet . . . why had he looked at me that way? What was he implying?

Stupidly I told him, "I am a levelheaded woman, Lord Rothesay, and I assure you that I would not tempt you in any way!" I did not add that because he was practically married to another, he had no right to even *suggest* what his feelings might be. Still he might be a rogue, and his statement indicative of his waggishness!

Whatever had caused him to say what he had, and despite my pleading with him to let me go only two weeks ago, I knew I could not leave yet. Just a few more days, a few more days until I find something . . . And then I will leave forever. Indeed, it will be a relief to get out of this sinister place!

October 22: While preparations are in full swing all around me for the annual All Hallows' Eve celebration, I have been overseeing the archaeological dig on the south inner curtain wall. Though this wall once rose thirty-five feet, like the other three, it is now almost level in places. We have cleared a space and have begun digging under the wall itself.

So far we have found evidence that indicates, without doubt, the timber structures that once existed here: a kitchen and storerooms, a postern gate, soldiers' barracks, and to my unrestrained delight, a well!

There is so much to study. We've found a miscellany of exciting relics: a stone Roman milestone, several brass pots, a washbasin, a copper bell, a metal belt buckle, and so on. By tomorrow, if my calculations are correct, we should begin digging in the southwest corner, where I believe the well is located.

However, I personally plan to spend most of tomorrow searching the wall of the oubliette, where Margaret was imprisoned, hoping to find more writings. Because the dungeons are in the lowest section of the structure, I may be able to measure the foundation down there and get an approximate date on the original building.

The marquess approached me again today. How handsome he looked in his stylish reefer and leather boots, but he did not notice me or allude to our previous conversation. How cool a man who would hint that he had feelings for me, could hurt me because of their power, and then act as if nothing had been said! I wonder if I read him wrong . . . ?

Yet, yet . . . oh, it is so wrong to say this, to put down on paper proof of my covetous feelings, but this is it: I am very attracted to the marquess! Sometimes I think it is only I who feels the magnetism, and of course, I must act as though I feel nothing! But whenever I see him, something catches at my heart. He is such a striking man in every sense, but there is no room to feel what I feel.

Pretending that I was unaffected by his presence, I discussed our dig at the south wall, and he listened intently, smiling with appreciation. I thought our conversation was finished when he grabbed my arm and told me, again, that he wanted me to go. The sooner the better!

I answered him in my best no-nonsense manner. Sometimes his intense nature makes him forget what is involved.

"But sir, you must remember the jewels! How much do you want to see them unveiled? Because it is only a matter of days before we find them."

His face grew dark and brooding, and he watched the distant activity at the dig site. He is most unsettling when he withdraws into himself, and I looked away.

Finally he turned back to me and said, "You are right, of course, but I beg you to work as fast as possible. I don't want your life endangered any more than it already is!" And he walked away.

What a strange and sinister-sounding warning! It was good that I was worked up into a state of fevered fancy since I would need all my energy for the stretch of work that lay ahead.

I am becoming more and more intrigued by him, and I must stop my daydreams!

More tomorrow night, for now I must fall into bed from pure exhaustion.

October 23: A horrible thing happened today. I am still breathless with the wonder of it! I am barely coherent enough to put pen to paper, but here is my story.

I was working by torchlight in the grim oubliette, rinsing the walls with a mild solvent. It seems that no other writing exists, and if it ever did, the markings are too faint to be discerned.

Next I decided to measure the foundation and was just leaving the murky chamber to fetch a measuring tool of mine—located in the Medieval Gallery, where all the old torture devices are stored—when a grating sound filled the air, and the iron-grilled portcullis, complete with spikes, crashed down and trapped me in the oubliette! I could have been killed!

Locked in the cell for many hours, I had plenty of time to think, believe me! Perhaps the marquess is right, and I should leave immediately. Was this falling mechanism an accident? How could such a ponderous piece of equipment come unhinged after all these centuries at the precise moment that I was underneath?

I had to tell myself that someone does not want me alive, does not want me to find the jewels! But I am stubborn—perhaps dangerously so, and though I wanted to crumble with fear, I knew in that instant that I would not give up until I had found the jewels.

As if reminding me how precarious my existence really is, a shadow passed before me in front of the fallen gate. It looked like a hooded monk from some long-dim past! And I knew it was the same priest that Victoria and her friend had seen!

Shuddering in terror, I was unable to scream, unable to move or even breathe! I know now what it means to *expire from fear!*

I knew why the figure was there before it even left me: it had released the gate in an attempt to impale me with the spikes. If I could uncover this priest's identity, I would know who to avoid—a good idea but probably impossible.

After an interminable time the marquess found me. I was closer to hysterics than I had ever been in my life, and he half carried, half walked me back to my quarters in the weaver's cottage. He quickly supplied me with a very old brandy from his cellars, and I was revived.

He didn't leave for a while, but instead started a fire, then threw himself on the settee. He smoked and stared out the window at the keep, not saying a word, not even moving. He looked as though he had seen a ghost, too. He sat there brooding, and I wanted to go to him so badly and tell him I could comfort him, but I didn't! Thank the Lord I did not! I showed my self-restraint this evening, but how long can I hold back? How long?

Finally he got up and left, bidding me good-bye with a slight gesture of his hand.

I haven't slept since, and now it is two o'clock in the morning. I could have kept him here with me all night! We share the same opinion, the same views. It would have been so pleasant. . . . And now, neither mind nor body is ready for sleep. I may sit in the window and wait for the sea gulls to come and pick about the courtyard. Or maybe I should read to fill these silent hours.

No, I will take some more laudanum, since it is the only cure for my insomnia.

October 27: I have been ill again. My head has throbbed for two days, my stomach is queasy, my mouth dry, and I have been seized with chills and fever. I am in no shape to return to work yet, but the marquess has reported that the well has been uncovered!

The Haunting of Victoria

The archaeologists are still in the process of cleaning out its wooden frame. Each chink of rubble, each stone fragment is taken out one at a time, washed, and examined closely. It is a painstaking process.

Victoria sits with me today by my fire. A penetrating cold wind is blowing from the sea, and it is said that the first frost will come early this year.

She has heard about my unfortunate entrapment and is frightened for me. She is watching me now while I make this entry in my diary, and has recommended that I hide it! Especially since my notes reveal beliefs about where the jewels may be hidden. Imagine, hiding this! But maybe the girl is right. I don't know. I don't know . . .

October 28: I have had a monumentally productive day! Amid the commotion and clamor of the servants' hanging banners and lanterns about the grounds for the big upcoming celebration, I worked closely with the archaeologists. We have cleaned out three quarters of the well already! I estimate that by day's end tomorrow, the well will be completely cleared. But still no sign of jewelry. No trace of anything, except chunks of mortar.

I have finally finished measuring the foundation in order to date the original keep. It appears to have been built around 1080 when William of Normandy took over the land, rebuilding the castle from the original fortress. I am coming up with a wealth of knowledge about the castle's history, and tomorrow I will write a report about my findings so far. The marquess plans to add a supplementary section at the back of the treatise, using my information.

October 29: I have finished my report, and when I took it to the marquess in his study, he told me to sit down. His face was white, but I said nothing and patiently waited for him to speak.

"If you do not leave by the end of the month, then you will give me no choice but to escort you on your way. I have already purchased a ticket for passage back to America."

I felt as though he had slapped me! And the very quiet, steady way in which he spoke made his news somehow harder to take. His tone was unyielding; his order not for debate.

I was subdued when I answered, but he could not see the tears that burned behind my eyes or hear the crack in my voice!

"If it is your wish to let me go, I cannot argue. You are my employer, after all. But I would ask for your complete cooperation the next two days in order that I may complete as much of my work as possible before leaving."

The bleakness that hung about him lightened a little, and he agreed, almost heartily, to give me unconditional support in order to step up my schedule.

How heavy is my heart, but I cannot dwell on useless emotions. Especially since they cannot change my destiny. Besides I will not jeopardize my life any longer!

This evening, the well has been cleared completely, and there is no trace of any kind of gem. How could I have been so wrong? All signs point to the well. I will go over my notes tonight. I cannot give up yet, not while two precious days are left to me.

October 30: I have been up all night, and my eyes are burning holes in their sockets, but I have discovered what I have so clumsily missed before! I am beside myself with joy, for I know now, most definitely, where there is a second well!

I have decided not to tell anyone of my discovery, for I am afraid that to divulge my secret may put my life in further jeopardy. No one will know about my new calculations! And if I do find something in the next twenty-four hours, what a surprise it will be for the marquess!

Now I will set down on paper what I have found. Believing that only one well existed, I was too stubborn

The Haunting of Victoria 139

to consider that perhaps another much earlier well had been built. According to the treatise, the Romans built a structure that, indeed, existed on Tavistock land but was positioned differently than the current castle.

The lighthouse was actually enclosed in the palisade around those first earthworks, so it is in that area I must search. Around the lighthouse are all kinds of stone rubble, indicating ruins of early buildings. I began to think that among those unobtrusive ruins there must exist another well. A fortification is always dependent on its water supply.

And why else would the priest be wandering about the lighthouse? And the tunnel—that we have finally cleared—leads from the dungeons directly into the lighthouse!

Some inchoate memory tugged at me. I vaguely remembered one of the technical drawings that the marquess had procured while in London. He had given me a stack of papers to peruse, and I had carefully placed them in a notebook. I had read them, studied them, gaining any further information about the dangerous times of the Inquisition, about the Rothesays themselves, about the political climate. And all of this information was greatly enlightening, for none of it existed in the treatise!

It was among those papers that my clue existed. Thankfully no one had access to the notebook but the marquess and myself. I pulled it off my shelf and quickly skimmed through it.

It wasn't long before I found what I was looking for. There, before my very eyes, was a copy of what a medieval builder believed were the plans for the Roman fort! A well-house tower had once existed on the very spot where William of Normandy built his lighthouse! Imagine, right on the highest point of land, William's builders constructed their lighthouse. It was happenstance that the crumbling well was below it! Somewhere ... somewhere in the lighthouse's stony foundation there was an entrance to that buried well. It told me as much in the black-and-white print!

I tried to subdue my excitement long enough to notice the other buildings of that early stronghold: there had been a hall, chapel, divers chambers, a gallery, a kitchen, brewery, bakery, and a sort of office or counting house.

I am going to the marquess as soon as the sun rises. I am so excited by this development that it is with effort that I stop to write this. I will not divulge to him what I have learned, but will insist that he respect my wishes to be left alone today. After all, he agreed to let me do as I pleased before leaving.

It shouldn't be hard to grant my request since the archaeologists are still digging at the south curtain wall, and thankfully there is enough confusion with tomorrow night's party that no one else will notice my movements.

October 31: Yesterday I painstakingly picked and shoveled at a small section of the lighthouse foundation. I spent the day digging, digging, and luckily the only person to spy me was Victoria! It was too hard to contain myself; I had to tell the girl. Had to confide in her my secret. That I was sure there was a well here, and that it was the hiding place of the jewels!

She was very pleased and spent the rest of the afternoon with me. At the end of the day I uncovered a rotting timber that belonged to the sides of an early well! I sent Victoria home to bed—to her extreme dismay—but I had a kerosene lamp to work by, and faltering from exhaustion, I finally uncovered the opening to the ancient well! I have found it!

I slept a few hours this morning in order to restore my vitality, and Victoria spent the whole afternoon with me again. We have been cleaning out the well, but not so carefully as we cleaned the first one. I am in a hurry, and if I make no discovery by tomorrow, I will be gone. So we are throwing out the debris, as clumsily as workmen discarding soil while digging a foundation.

I ate an early dinner and now evening is falling. Carriages are drawing up to the front gates, eerily glowing

The Haunting of Victoria

jack-o'-lanterns illuminate the landscape, and an atmospheric fog clings round the cheerfully lit castle.

I am hastily jotting down these last few words before I rush out to my secret well again to begin my last day's digging! Victoria has assured me that she can find a suitable hiding place for my diary until I return for it in the morning. With all the guests here, and everyone dressed in fantastic guises, who can tell how safe it would be lying about in the open!

Before I go, one last comment. Though it pains me not a little to pen this paragraph, the marquess's choice of costume is rather unfortunate.

Victoria has just told me what the mistress and master are wearing tonight. Margaret is dressed as the goddess Diana, wearing a linen chiton and woolen cloak. She is carrying a little jeweled bow and arrow to aim playfully at the marquess's heart. He, though, is not dressed as a Roman god. He is wearing the awful black robes and hooded cape of a sixteenth-century priest!

Tonight, as I go to the deserted ruins, I am more afraid than I have been so far.... But I must not think of my fears, for tomorrow the jewels will be restored to the family, and I will be gone from this place.

The diary ended there, but I knew what had happened. I extinguished the lamp and, lying back on the settee, closed my eyes. I was awake for the rest of the night.

Chapter Eleven

IT IS MERCIFUL that memory blots out pain, emotion, so that those living with a great shock or turmoil can still function with a semblance of normalcy. As scenes unfold one acts out of reflex, as though possessing no emotional life. And so it was with me.

With the diary safely hidden under my mattress in my room, the bears stuffed in several hatboxes, I continued my routine. I rose early the next morning; Victoria and I breakfasted together in the schoolroom, after which Victoria returned to her painting so she could finish today; and we spent the early afternoon at our easels. It was coincidence that I had chosen the lighthouse as my subject. But now as I surveyed my gloomy canvas washed with gray tones, I felt I must have known something all along....

Not until a beaming Victoria held up her canvas with a proud flourish did I regain full control of my senses. I blinked at the startling picture before approaching her and taking the painting to get a better look. Only an instant passed before it dropped from my hands like a hot coal.

As a painting, it was not only brilliantly rendered, it had caught Catherine's likeness like no other picture I had seen. Victoria had captured the precise lines of my sister's features: narrow nose, dark, arched brows, full lips, a subtle hardening of her almond-shaped eyes, hair pulled severely up on her head.

She was no longer dressed in old-fashioned clothes, but wore a simple lace collar and a fitted bodice. The opulent jewels were even more showy against her plain dress, around her bare wrists. They looked gaudy and gimcrack.

Behind her bare neck was a midnight-black hand, reaching out for her, ready to touch her soft skin beneath the scintillating cascade of stones that hung there! Above the hand was a faceless head, the treacherous cowl framing it.

"Oh!" I exhaled, bending down to retrieve the silent Catherine, who stared up impassively at me.

Victoria's wide eyes surveyed me without guile. Why had she painted Catherine twice? Unless . . . she wanted to reveal the priest's identity, and by using Catherine as her subject she reenacted a scene that actually took place!

A gripping terror coursed through me. Did this mean that she had *seen* the priest touch my sister? Did Catherine, in fact, wear the jewels and were they plucked diabolically from her neck? I trembled on the brink of a revelation. Incredibly it seemed that Victoria's paintings were exposing what her mind refused to acknowledge. That she, indeed, knew who the malevolent priest was, and she was using pictures, instead of words, to tell her story! I wondered what her next portrait would reveal.

Holding the painting with an unsteady hand, I pulled a crayon and tablet toward me with the other, and wrote: *Do you know who wears this priest's robe? Who might be the person masquerading as the phantom, wandering about at night? If you know, Victoria, tell me before anyone else finds out. Do not expose what you know to anyone but me! I am your friend!*

I waited a terrifying moment for her reply. But she merely looked at me, her eyes luminous in the afternoon light. She slowly picked up her crayon.

I do not know, Miss Durnham. Perhaps it is no person, but an actual ghost!

If I could have shouted at her, my voice would have risen to hysteria. As it was, I could only grasp the crayon with a maniacal grip and write.

Surely you don't believe it is a ghost! Victoria, I ask you again, do you know? Your knowledge could save both our lives!

With the quick temper of a spoiled child, she picked up the crayon and broke it in two. She scowled at me in protest and scribbled: *No, I do not know!*

She pushed the paper away and, snatching the portrait from me, stomped back to her easel and hid the picture under a piece of fabric she was using for a still life. It was better stowed away so that no one could see how near she was to the haunting truth! I glanced at her. She had tossed a new wood frame on the floor and was stretching a canvas over it, hammering tacks around its edges.

Realizing I had hurt her with my pressing queries, I scrawled an apology to her. *Victoria, I did not mean to offend you. Your painting is lovely. You are truly an artist.*

She turned to me, her black look subsiding. Again I felt her scrutiny, as I had the night of the ball. She wrote: *Why are you here? To teach me to paint? Or are there other reasons?*

I tried not to falter. *Of course, I am here to teach you.*
Then why do you look like Miss Ryce? When you wear your hair pulled back in a knot, you resemble her!

I reeled. How many others had seen this resemblance? Had the marquess? It was ridiculous to let the girl frighten me so!

You perhaps see a similarity that many American women have to one another, I lied, *a certain style that makes us resemble each other even though our features are different.*

I admonished Victoria for letting her imagination run away with her, but my plea looked pitifully weak on paper. We continued writing notes back and forth until she became pensive and agreed that perhaps my similarity to Catherine had been a coincidence after all. Suddenly I looked up to find Eva standing there, a disapproving frown upon her face.

"I haven't seen the household in such a state of disruption since . . . that historian disappeared."

I felt my face pale. "Whatever do you mean by that remark?"

Instead of answering, she handed me a sealed envelope.

"It's from the master. He requests an answer immediately."

She watched me carefully as I opened the note with trembling fingers, the blood rushing hotly through my veins.

Dear Miss Durnham (Anne):

I am hoping that I am not sending this invitation too late. It is imperative that you meet me at the lighthouse at four o'clock for the afternoon's tour I am conducting. I believe you will be interested in some of the history, and there is a matter of great urgency concerning Victoria.

Yours,
James Rothesay

The note was scrawled in a tearing hurry. He tried to make it sound as if I would enjoy the tour, but the tone carried the unmistakable authority of a summons. And the mention of Victoria alerted me to danger, more than I cared to admit.

I closed the letter and kept my eyes lowered.

"Madam, it is urgent that you answer right away. He is waiting in his study for me to tell him what you have decided."

I looked up at her. Waiting in his study! Of course, he was eager. He had trapped Catherine into finding the jewels for him. Now I was his next victim, since my urging Victoria to paint was bringing the girl dangerously close to unveiling the priest's identity!

"I will go," I said, meeting Eva's direct gaze.

"Thank you, madam, that is all." She shot Victoria a quick, concerned glance before leaving.

I trembled. There was a spider at the center of his shining web . . . a malignancy festering at the very core of this house! And it was the king himself! Catherine had fallen in love with him, as I was trying not to do. She tried to subdue her fervor, her longing for the marquess, and somehow I felt she was informing me to do the same.

The mantel clock struck three with a cheerful little sound. Galvanized into activity by my knowledge of the lateness of the day, I stood, smoothing my skirts. I would go to the lighthouse now and take a quick look around before the marquess arrived.

If Catherine was still alive, I was her last hope. She might be gasping her last breath, and there was no time to lose. I would check the lighthouse, the ruins. Next the church, the keep, the cellars again.

If Catherine was not alive . . . I must discover where she had gone—before the ghost priest found Victoria's new painting and turned on her! The girl knew too much, possibly everything, and there was no doubt that her life was in grave danger.

I hastily wrote Victoria a message: *Victoria, there is one small detail on the lighthouse that I must check in order to complete my painting. And then I will accompany the marquess for a tour. I will be away for several hours. Can you manage alone for a while?*

She read my note and seemed agreeable. She answered that she would be here, working on a new painting all afternoon.

I put on my cape and went swiftly out the door.

The afternoon sun was strong and warming. The rain of the day before had washed the world, and the air was pure and blue. The sea below the chalk cliffs was gentle, and the greening downs spread before me like a velvet blanket.

I strode with purposeful steps toward the lighthouse, the ruins surrounding it. My heart leaped uncomfortably, and I shivered, though the breeze was mild.

"Catherine, Catherine, I am so close!" I exhaled, placing a tentative hand on the stony exterior of the lighthouse.

I walked through the arched doorway and looked around.

"It's so small!" I thought aloud, glancing up the side of one wall at the narrow stairs, the tiny wooden platform on the top. The sight of it sent a whispering chill down the back of my neck.

My look appraised the floor of the structure. Tile met walls at uneven intervals. The mortar between stones was flaking and cracking, especially at the bottom. There were holes caused by this, but hardly one large enough to lead to an entrance to a ruin!

The only lead I had was Catherine's mention of a rotting timber somewhere close to the foundation. I pulled my cotton skirts about my knees and squatted on all fours. This was going to be the hardest part of the job.

Luckily I had a paint knife stuck in my skirt pocket, and pulling it out, I began poking at the gaps underneath the walls. By some miracle I found a place where the mortar looked darker, fresher!

My hands shook, and my ears were alert to sounds as I chipped at it. All the while I kept turning over in my mind what must have happened to Catherine. If she found the jewels, did the priest follow her to take them as Victoria's painting suggested? And then had he covered up the opening with a new mixture of sand and lime? All I knew for certain was that she had disappeared on the night of All Hallows' Eve . . . when the marquess masqueraded as a priest!

Though the mortar appeared to be recently applied, it was stronger than was first evident, and I could not budge it with my knife. I would have to come later, with a stronger tool. Perhaps tonight or tomorrow night when the moon shone to light the way . . .

There was a crunch of footsteps nearby, and in the sleepy afternoon peace, they sounded as loud as gunshots. I stayed hunkered down, crouching against the wall, like a hare in her burrow. Dizzy with panic, I watched the doorway in agonizing silence.

A silhouette of a large man appeared suddenly, blocking out the cheerful light. His breathing was hard and loud, as if he had been running. The black topper, his broad shoulders, the strong build made me gasp. It was the marquess, of course.

I held my breath, waiting for something to happen. Then the figure took one careful step into the room. Then another. Because he was backed against the light, I couldn't see his face, but his fist was clenched menacingly around a shovel.

My heart stampeded in my chest. What was he doing with that deadly-looking tool?

He stopped walking, and I saw that his jacket was the official red English coat of a warden. It wasn't the marquess at all, but Hal, the gatekeeper!

Thinking it better not to wait for his discovery of me, I rose to my feet. He was startled at my sudden movement and swung around to face me.

My hands were clenched so tightly around the stiff material of my skirts, they almost tore it. My lips were dry and barely moved.

"Hello," I said hoarsely. "I . . . hope I didn't startle you."

He moved a step closer to me. I could see his face now, and it was etched with astonishment and, underlying that, rage.

"I could say the same to you," he said gruffly.

"No . . . you didn't startle me," I said, protesting far too much. "I was only looking at the walls, you see, I am painting a picture of the lighthouse." I touched the cold stone to emphasize my point. "And I needed to make sure my calculations were correct."

My voice cracked, and he stared at me disbelieving. I could not meet his look, but glanced instead at the shiny medals hanging on one shoulder of his jacket.

He came nearer and leaned on his shovel, cornering me against the wall. He knew he had me trapped, and not for the first time since my arrival, a consuming terror gripped me. It would be so easy for him to raise the shovel, to strike me.

My hands were clenched in trembling little fists as tight as a hawk's claws. "Well, I'll be getting back to Victoria now," I said.

And as I moved to get around him his hand reached out and clamped down on my arm. On some half-conscious level I knew I had to subdue the violence that lit his eyes. He was breathing rapidly again, and I smelled alcohol on his breath.

"Why are you really here, little lady?"

The Haunting of Victoria   149

I panicked. I might be lucky enough to wriggle free, make a wild dash for the door, or . . . I could bring up the subject of the jewels to measure his reaction.

I met his glazed look and heard myself stammer foolishly, "Why, of course, to find the famous Rothesay jewels! Why else would I be here!" I attempted a rueful laugh, but it sounded like a cough.

His bleary brown eyes came closer to mine, his hand tightening on my arm. "You . . . you'd better go, Miss Durnham. Before it's too late!"

I reevaluated the situation. Perhaps I should struggle to loosen his grip. His sour breath was revolting, and a quick flood of annoyance and fear burst through me. I yanked hard to get away, but he held me fast.

"I will tell the master about you!" I threatened, knowing full well that my threats could not frighten such a man.

A gleam of anger flared in his cold chestnut eyes before he masked his reaction with a mirthless grin.

"I don't think this is the time for complaints, Miss Durnham. You've already stirred up things enough around here!"

"What do you mean?" I asked.

"It's pretty obvious, isn't it?" he hissed. "The girl is painting strange pictures. The master and mistress are at odds with each other, and now the . . . the wedding has been changed from a big ceremony to a small affair in the little chapel this Friday! Your influence is no good."

His words, slurred in that odd accent I had detected in him before, caused my heart to beat wildly. I wanted to toss back an impertinent remark, but could think of none.

My influence? Yes . . . hadn't Eva implied that I had been disrupting the family home? Yes, Victoria was painting incriminating pictures, but what had I done to make the master and mistress change their wedding plans? Unless Margaret became jealous of the marquess's attentions toward me and stepped up the date? No, that was too absurd to be true.

His clasp on my arm was as tight as a vise as he began uttering words of warning. I reeled at the stench of his liquored breath and suppressed a cry of pain.

"Only disaster can be-befall you, my naive little lady, because someone doesn't like what you are doing!" he spat.

"Let go of me this instant or I will scream!"

A shadow darkened the room. I jerked around to glance at the door, and the gatekeeper dropped my arm abruptly.

In the doorway, framed by the blue sky, stood the marquess. In a frenzied moment I controlled the urge to run into his arms and sob with unutterable relief. I stood stock-still and stared at him with a dazed expression. He stared back for a quick burning moment, as if to chastise me, before he glared at the gatekeeper.

For an instant I wondered if Rothesay could be a murderer. Did he plan to have Hal find me here? He had asked me to meet him here, after all. This had been his suggestion, his invitation.

Without further hesitation, Rothesay strode across the floor and grabbed my hand. He shot Hal a savage look that froze my blood, before turning to examine me.

"Are you all right?"

"Yes," I muttered softly. "I believe I am."

"If you ever lay a hand on her again, Mr. Mathews, I will have you deported so far away, Australia will seem close to home!" he snarled hotly.

"Yes, sir," Hal answered stiffly.

There was a gaping silence as Rothesay twisted his lips in barely suppressed fury. When he spoke, his words were edged with steel.

"Mr. Mathews, I'd recommend attending to your duties of cleaning up around the ruins right away—as I told you to do originally—and stay out of other people's business! The guests will be arriving soon."

His tone made me tremble, and I was glad that his anger was not aimed at me.

Before hearing Hal's answer, the marquess strengthened his hold on me and stormed out into the sunny day. My hand was crushed by his large one, and barely able to follow him, I ran in little leaps to keep up with his long, purposeful strides.

He led me away from the ruins, away from the keep, toward the white chalk cliffs and the shimmering sea below...

A million thoughts burst in my brain, but none of them shouted danger. His attention was completely upon me, he watched me, observed me, and there was no unkindness about him. At least for now he meant me no harm.

We stopped in front of a scrubby line of yew hedge that blocked our view of the castle. The water was not more than a half mile in the distance, deep green and glistening in the sunlight. It carried the moist scent of salt spray, and the fresh aroma exhilarated me. The sand, chalky white like the cliffs and lined with pale, smooth undulations, lay invitingly below us.

"Anne," he said quietly, and the sound of my name on his lips made me tremble.

I turned to him.

He was dressed in a fine suit of English tweed, the dark specks of color enhancing his black, compelling eyes. He watched me solemnly, and I felt an irrepressible passion mounting within me.

He reached out, putting his hand around my waist, drawing me slowly to him. For a whirring moment I knew I should resist, but his tempestuous gaze was on me, inviting me to surrender. For that brief span of time I was no more than his willing victim, and I submitted gladly.

The restraint he had shown so far vanished rapidly, and his grip on me tightened; he kissed my mouth hard, unyieldingly, with a fervor and brutal strength that I had only guessed he might possess. There are no words to describe how his lips on mine made me reel, spin under his powerful embrace. Desire began to course through my veins as though he stoked the red-hot embers within.

His hands were in my hair, pulling out the pins, feeling its texture, letting it fall around my shoulders. He touched me first gently, then with urgency. His fingers brushed my cheek tenderly, my neck, then grazed a sizzling path down to my collarbone. He whispered my name again in a throaty whisper. And I heard my own stunned voice rasp out, "James..."

I raised my eyes to find his gaze on me, filled with dark desire, and suddenly a quick, irrational fear spurred me to utter a cry of protest, and I forced myself away from his powerful grasp. What else must surely follow?

"No, we mustn't! Not while... not when you are to be married!" I exhaled, watching him.

He stood, arms flung down at his sides, not moving, only staring bleakly beyond me. "Yes, married." His eyes were on the beach below us.

"I've heard the date is changed," I said with grim resolution.

"The ceremony will take place in three days." His voice was flat.

I swallowed hard.

"I'm sorry," he said softly, meeting my look again. "But not about the kiss. I would say that it was all a mistake, except that it isn't. I had every intention of kissing you, just as I've wanted to kiss you since the first moment I laid eyes on you."

There was no suitable reply to that.

He stepped close to me. "I've never known a woman like you, Anne. How could I guess that when I sent for a tutor to my niece, I would be receiving an answer to my prayers?"

I met his somber look. It was frightening how much I wanted to believe him!

"I am glad for you," I said stiffly, turning away.

He touched my chin and tilted my head to him. I thought he would kiss me again, but his thumb and forefinger held me, forcing me to look into his stormy eyes.

"You've heard rumors, haven't you? About what a blackguard I am."

"Not rumors, exactly."

"They're all true, you should listen to them." He released me, picking up a twig and throwing it far down below.

I watched his tortured profile, disconsolate, gloomy. "Everyone knows that I used to come here often...

The Haunting of Victoria

with the historian from America. She was a bright girl, very much like you."

I was glad he was looking away from me.

"And when she . . . well, disappeared, I was naturally blamed. The papers hinted that there had been foul play, but no proof of my guilt has ever surfaced. So for all we know I may still be a murderer."

"Only if the woman is . . . dead," I replied raggedly.

He shot me a bold glance. "Ah! So you believe she is still alive? I wish that were true, how I wish that were true!"

I bit my lip and tasted blood.

"Ever since her disappearance, I have felt so lost, felt such an emptiness that could not be filled no matter how hard I tried. Strangely enough I hardly knew Miss Ryce. But I understood her. Do you know what I mean? And so it is with you. You two are very different, but yet . . . yet I could swear that you are alike, swear that the same thread links you two in some vital way."

He paused; then: "Not until I met you did I realize how deep my longing had been. Did I comprehend the full extent of the happiness I have been missing."

The blood pounded into my face until the roots of my hair burned. He picked up another twig and tossed it.

"I know people still say that I induced her into finding the jewels for me, before . . . disposing of her. But I did not." His voice lowered. "For where is my fortune, then? And why would I harm the woman I was so fond of?"

He turned and appraised me. I shrugged my shoulders helplessly, trying to feign indifference.

"The truth is hard to hear, isn't it?"

I met his look, my heart bursting, but I could only shake my head numbly.

"I can see that you are full of doubts about me. That is why I did not want to confess these things to you. If I thought you cared . . . only a little." His voice was going deep.

I could hardly contain my madly careening emotions!

"How can I answer that?" The words toppled out before I could stop them. "Whatever I said would be a lie."

He frowned, but he didn't reply.

"It would be a lie if I told you that I didn't care, a lie if I said I could throw all caution to the winds and care for you completely." My voice was husky with emotion.

"That is all I can hope for now," he said in an undertone.

The tide was beginning to come in, and we stood, side by side, not facing each other, watching the surge of the waters. After a while he took my hand and squeezed it gently.

"The tour will start soon, and I need to be at the church to welcome the guests. Though I love to see your hair cascading around your shoulders, I will help you pin it on your head again. May I?"

"Yes," I answered by reflex.

With the same tenderness that I had seen him display with Victoria, he gathered my hair into his hands, and guided by my own hands, he replaced the clips. I felt the warmth of his body as he stood close behind me, absorbed in his task. How strong was the urge to drag his hands from my head, to pull them tightly around me, to feel his intoxicating kisses on my neck!

When I was made to look presentable again, he stepped away from me and smiled. "You are so lovely." He sighed. "I hope you will still join me for the tour?"

I turned away, wanting to say no, but my lips quivered wordlessly instead.

He placed his forefinger over my mouth. "Say nothing. Not yet. Not before I tell you why I really brought you here. And then you can answer if you want to spend any more time with a bad lot like me."

I glanced at him and was glad with every fiber of my being that he had kissed me. And I knew that I would do it again . . .

"I'm afraid the gatehouse keeper is right," he was saying grimly. "Your life is in imminent danger. And so is my niece's. I think it best that you and Victoria move out of here until the . . . the wedding is over." He faced me so swiftly, so earnestly that I wondered if he, too, had seen Victoria's second painting!

The Haunting of Victoria

"Anne, I can hardly explain what I wish I could tell you now." He took my hands in his. "I am not a good man. But you know that now."

I felt a great stir of emotion. "Who am I to pass judgment on somebody's goodness? We are all different parts good and bad."

"How simple you make it sound," he said.

"Human nature is never simple."

He didn't answer, but let go of my hands.

We were walking back along the cliffs, out of the hedge, toward the church again, where we stopped.

"I would like you to prepare yourself and Victoria to leave tomorrow night. After sunset."

His face clouded, and his voice did not hide the urgency he felt. It would be so easy to do as he told me, but what if I was walking into a trap? And he was not protecting us at all? Still I could not disagree with what he said.

"If you think it wise for us to hide, I will agree to your plan. I have worried about Victoria's safety for many days now. I, too, am afraid, but more for the girl than for myself."

"Then meet me at your rooms immediately after the tour, and I will give you all the details. I trust you to follow my plan implicitly in order for you and Victoria to escape unharmed." He looked at me with great tenderness, but refrained from touching me. "I cannot bear to think what may become of you if you stay. If something happens to you because of my clumsiness, as it did with Miss Ryce, I will go mad with regret and loneliness!"

His eyes were dark, but glints of light danced in the brown around his irises. He brushed the unruly tendril of hair away from his forehead.

"And what happens when I return?" I queried.

"That is something I cannot tell you. Not now. Can you hang on for me? Will you promise not to give up on what I can only call my selfish intentions, if I tell you that you will be rewarded? That I will give you all I have?"

Of course! He will marry someone else but keep me as his concubine, his mistress. Just as he had intended to do with Catherine.

I asked boldly, "Are you asking me to be your mistress?"

"I am not a scoundrel, Anne, whatever you may think."

"But how can I believe your intentions are honorable when you are marrying Margaret?"

His eyes raked over me. "I cannot ask you to believe anything. Especially now, in light of the wedding. What I can ask, is that you trust me."

I looked away and felt the sharp sting of tears behind my eyes. "I'm afraid that will be hard to do," I said thickly.

"I understand," he said dismally. "I have agonized over what I would say to you when the time comes. I thought at first I would ask you to run away with me, but you would think I was impetuous and a rogue."

"Yes, that's true."

"And I knew that if I told you I need you and want you to stay forever, you would only flee."

"Yes."

"Anne, when you and Victoria return to Tavistock, I cannot force you to stay, but promise me in the meanwhile you will think about what I have said."

"What good can come of an adulterous relationship?"

He reeled back, hurt playing all over his face. "You are right, of course. It's a grim offer at best. Right now I can offer you no more. But tomorrow may be different. That's what I want you to think about. What *may* be."

"That will not be hard to do," I said wistfully, an unbearable longing taking possession of me.

I was suddenly aware that several men were waving at us from the ruins. In that same instant he noticed them, too, and waving back, turned to me.

"The guests are here. You will accompany me?"

I thought of all he knew about the castle's history, all that Catherine had discovered for him, and I wanted to know more about the lighthouse.... "Yes, I would like that," I said.

The Haunting of Victoria 157

"Come on, then." He caught my elbow and escorted me. "We must not delay any longer. My guests are waiting."

In silence we made our way back to the lighthouse, where the tour was beginning.

Glancing around, I saw that Hal was nowhere in sight. A few excited ladies, dressed in handsome walking suits and carrying lace parasols, joined the gentlemen, and the marquess took a place in front of them. I stood behind the couples, wondering how I had gotten caught in such a situation. The marquess surely hadn't kissed me passionately and whispered words of love. No, surely that had happened to someone else. . . .

A wave of laughter assaulted me. The guests were smiling at something the marquess said. I was riveted to attention and began listening.

His manner was smooth, his voice well modulated and even. He talked about how he was an architect by profession, talked about his ancestors, about Tavistock's history, but I gleaned nothing new from his speech.

As the tour progressed I followed the tourists into the church, learning about its history, then through the greening yard and around the gardens, where early flowers, bright in the sun, were showing their silky heads. The others were busy asking questions; I only marveled at the man to whom I was fatally attracted.

His charismatic personality induced the guests to relax and feel comfortable in the great span of walkways and gardens that surrounded his stone fortress. Thankfully the tour was short, and while the guests were departing happily I found a suitable moment to make an inconspicuous exit.

I was turning the handle of the door to my rooms when the marquess raced up behind me.

He caught me by the arm and spun me around. "I'm sorry for this haste, but I will be away tomorrow and, anyway, for your safety I want everything settled tonight."

He thrust a burlap bag into my hand. "Here are a few necessities for your escape. Candles, matches, a map."

It was impossible to disregard the touch of excitement, the thrill of adventure that made me tremble. There was no doubt that danger surely followed, however, and I swallowed down the fear that rose suddenly in my throat.

"You and Victoria must leave at the stroke of midnight. Tomorrow night." He extricated the map.

"Now, here"—he pointed to a dark *X* that indicated Tavistock—"this is where the castle is located in relation to town. First, leave your tower and exit through the King's Gate. It is the main entrance, as you know."

"Yes," I replied numbly. "Right under the gatehouse."

He glanced at me knowingly. "The lane leading out from there passes on through neighboring hops gardens, toward town. This is the road you and Victoria will take. Do not light the candle unless it is absolutely necessary. I don't want you to call attention to yourselves."

Yes, I thought, nodding. A beacon of light to show the priest our way . . .

"After almost two kilometers, you will pass an abandoned stone castle, in ruins. It is set on the cliffs over the sea, but there is a stone approach to the keep on the landward side. There, on the drive, you will find a carriage waiting for you. The driver will take you and Victoria to an apartment in the Royal Albion Hotel located in Dover. You must never leave your rooms and keep the shutters closed. Your food will be brought to you. You must go nowhere until I fetch you."

A door shut somewhere above us, and I shuddered. He looked up and back to me. His face was drawn, worry lines etched around his eyes.

"You will follow these instructions exactly?"

"Yes" I sighed. But would I?

Without warning he pulled me roughly into his arms and kissed me. His lips were ruthlessly selfish, taking all that was his. My desire kept pace with his own mounting passion, and I was limp, clinging to him, uncertain, ecstatic.

When he released me, his face was closed, somber. I waited, watching him, beginning to feel afraid again. What had we done? What was he thinking?

"I will come for you and Victoria at the hotel on Saturday." He brushed my cheek. "Until then . . ."

He turned around and walked away from me. I could only stare incredulously at his retreating form.

Chapter Twelve

VICTORIA WAS ASLEEP by the time I made my way back to her rooms. I placed my hand on her cool forehead; she was breathing evenly. I sniffed her chocolate—it smelled like cocoa and milk—and made sure the chair was wedged against the door of the secret entranceway. It might not keep the intruder out, but at least the screeching of the chair as it slid across the floor would alert me.

Finally I lay down, my head whirling. How frightening this was! I wanted so much to believe that I should wait for the marquess, that he cared for me, that he would find some last-minute way to avoid marriage to Margaret. But that was all part of my romantic dream.

I folded my arms behind my head and stared at the ceiling. It must have been hours that I lay awake before a singularly disquieting sound made adrenaline shoot through my system. My heart was beating in my throat. I listened. There was no noise of the chair moving by the paneled door. What did I hear, then? It was the main door to Victoria's bedroom! The knob was turning, turning slowly!

Hadn't I remembered to lock it? Surely I did, then how could someone open it? Unless the intruder had a key!

The door opened, spilling yellow lamp light from the hall. I was lying at the wrong angle to see who entered, and didn't dare move. My body was rigid as I held my breath and waited.

The door closed quickly with a menacing click. A soupy darkness fell on the room; the shutters were open, but the

The Haunting of Victoria 161

moon was covered by clouds. The hearth fire had died long ago.

Footsteps were making a slow progression toward Victoria and me. Suddenly something tumbled and fell on the floor. The walking stopped. Whatever had fallen was pushed aside, and the trespasser continued on his slow, deliberate way.

I heard breathing as he passed so closely by me I could have touched him. My eyes were adjusting to the darkness again, and I made out his trailing robe. It was undoubtedly the priest!

There was a pause of complete silence. I closed my eyes tightly, for the phantom stood directly over me! Watching me!

I waited. It was hair-raising turbulence in that hushed quiet. The hound was closing in.

There was no strike from a candlestick or shot from a gun. The priest crept on, his robe whispering across the carpet. My blood began to flow again, and I opened my eyes.

He stood against the window, the dun light framing his black silhouette as he hovered at Victoria's bedside. What should I do? I thought, clamped down against my pillow.

He stood there watching her, throwing a deeper shadow across the bed. He hovered for a moment, then mercifully left again, as suddenly as he had entered. He padded past me without stopping and opened the door, closing it softly behind him.

I was up, tearing off my dressing gown with trembling hands, pulling on my dress, my boots, my cape. My mind raced out of control, I couldn't think, was unable to make a decision, there were too many hurtful things to face. But I must follow that priest. For if it was the marquess, I could not trust him as he had begged, could not go where he had planned for Victoria and me to hide—but I would expose him as the ghost, as my sister's captor. And justice would be served.

The light flickered wildly in the hallway wall sconces as though disturbed by a movement. Unsure of where he might have passed, I trailed down the gloomy corridor, down the dim turning stairs, following my inclinations. At the bottom of the stairs, I listened for the sound of his footfall. Only the creaks and groans of the yawning house met my wary ears.

I stumbled along the narrow passage, illuminated by an occasional emerald tulip lamp. I reached the great pillared entrance, now deep in shadow.

My quick glance around told me that I had been foolish to come here. There was nothing, no trace of movement. I was about to turn away when my eyes spotted a glow of light under a door at the far end of the hall. With stealth, I moved toward it.

Stopping just outside, I pressed my face to the carved wood. There was no sound coming from within. I knocked very softly. No answer. A little louder. Still I heard nothing.

With muscles tensed, braced for disaster, I turned the doorknob. It gave with a tiny little screech that seemed to penetrate the farthest corners of the house. I stood inside the marquess's study.

A reading lamp burned brightly on the rolltop desk in the room's center. Two tiger skins sprawled on the carpets, their massive jaws wide and snarling, eyes alight with the glint of the attacker. In the enormous grate a new fire leaped and hissed. Books were heaped on the desk, on the floor, on the elaborately carved bookshelves lining the walls.

I made my way past a standing globe and maps on the wall and approached the desk. An ashtray with a smoldering pipe and ashes sat to one side. Its pungent aroma forced me to stifle a cough. Next to it were his steel-frame glasses, tossed there without a case.

It was apparent that he had just made a hasty exit. But from where? Not through the hall door. Could there be a hidden paneled door in the wall? Some sort of escape route?

Circling around the desk, I made for the far wall when something caught my eye. I swung around. His top desk drawer was partially open. Something black stuck out, and I went to it and pulled. A great piece of ebony material fell into my hands. With tiny bubbles of hysteria rising in my throat, I unfolded the stretch of fabric. Though I had expected it, goose pimples slid over my cold skin. It was, indeed, the hooded priest's robe!

I don't remember how I got back to Victoria's rooms. I must have flown there on wings, because before I knew what was happening, I was packing her things, preparing a new course of action.

For the rest of the endless night I sat on the edge of Victoria's bed, half-choked with fear and tears of desperation. I didn't want to believe what I had seen in the marquess's study; I wanted to go on trusting him blindly, cravenly, driven by instinct. I had kissed him, that much I could savor, but as for the rest . . . it was best forgotten.

By the time daybreak arrived, a touch of gray at first, then pale mother-of-pearl, I had bathed and dressed in a tulle smock with a jacket to match, and sturdy shoes. Victoria awoke, and when she saw her leather traveling bag open and full of her clothes, she looked at me as though she always awoke to find herself packed.

She reached to her bedside table and grabbed pad and pencil. *I had another bad dream last night. I thought I heard something crash to the floor, and when I opened my eyes, that hooded ghost stood close to me! Watching me!*

My nerves were taut as a wire, my heart in my throat.

I know, I wrote back. *Victoria, do you feel all right? Not sick or anything?*

Her eyes slid to the big tumbler of chocolate. *Yes, I am fine,* she wrote. Then after a moment, added: *I did not drink the chocolate. It had a nasty smell to it, so I threw it away last night.*

My hands were unsteady as I sat next to her and explained our dilemma, on paper.

That was smart of you. I have requested to see your mother, and I will go and get my bags in the meanwhile. We have to go away for a little while. We must hide until the ghost priest can be caught. Will you dress and be ready to leave when I return?

Her face, lifted to mine, looked small and pale. She nodded her head.

I turned to go, but she grabbed my wrist. *Wait, Miss Anne, I have finished another portrait for you. May I show you now?*

I was filled with a thrill of nervous horror and exhaled a murmur of apprehension. Before I could answer, she jumped out of bed, her diaphanous gown flowing around her like cobwebbed silk, and made for the corner where she had placed her easel.

When she held the small canvas up to me, I staggered back to the bed, staring in disbelief at the masterful rendering of myself!

I was depicted in the same regal pose as she had captured Catherine, head high, shoulders square, hair pulled up in a fanciful style and looped with pearls. My neck was bare down to a revealingly low bodice, a wide lace collar ran 'round the back of the dress, and draped over the woven black and gold of the gown hung those glittering, menacing gems! Lurking behind me in a velvety black robe stood the priest, the arm reaching out for my neck, the face hidden in transparent shadow.

I heard my voice exclaim, "Victoria!" when I heard the knock at the door.

I shot Victoria a worried glance and laid the picture facedown on her bed, calling to enter.

The door opened and Margaret rushed in, hugging a fur-trimmed robe about her person, shining hair flowing about her shoulders. It wasn't until she was halfway across the room that I noticed tears staining her face, her eyes red and swollen. My heart jumped.

I went to her, concern lacing my voice. "I asked Eva to request that I see you. But what has happened?"

Her look quickly took in Victoria, but she didn't go to her. "Is my daughter well? Is she safe?"

In that sizzling instant I knew she also feared for Victoria's life. "Yes, madam, I have made sure of that."

Her amber eyes fastened on me, wary, tired, scared. "Thank God," she muttered desperately. "I am so afraid," she began, fresh tears wetting her lashes.

The Haunting of Victoria

I offered her a handkerchief. She snatched it from me.

Gesturing toward the open trunk, which Margaret noticed for the first time, I said, "The ghost priest visited again last night, and I, too, am afraid—for the girl. I know I must take her somewhere, she is unsafe here. But I am uncertain where. That is why I called for you."

I thought for a moment she would faint. Her skin blanched, and she made a little scratching gesture at her throat.

"Madam, are you all right?"

She gulped and recovered her speech. "Yes, Miss Durnham. I'm fine, I . . . it's just that I knew it happened again . . . I knew the ghost came to my daughter's rooms last night. I went to look for James last night, and he was . . . he was gone."

It was my turn to pale.

"Please say nothing. Pretend that I have not told you anything about this. For none of us is safe. Do I have your word?"

"Yes."

"My fiancé cannot be trusted. I do not want this union with him. I am trying to behave properly, but I am doing a poor job. The wedding"—she paused, visibly struggling for the words—"will be held early. This Friday. It must take place, yet in my heart I do not want it to. This is not a good match for me, for us. He is a scoundrel, a rogue, and possibly even . . . oh, it doesn't matter."

I watched her, a mounting horror shadowing her features. "I am trapped by him. He cannot control his dark desires, his manly urges." She puckered her lips in repugnance. "He has had his way with me."

I lowered my glance, feeling as if she had struck me with her bold revelation.

"And now he is dangerous to Victoria. I fear . . ." She bit back new tears. "I fear he wants her out of the way."

I flinched, benumbed by her words. How wrong to think I was past surprise!

She continued. "I had the contents of Victoria's chocolate tested by my doctor. You know, the cup you brought?"

I nodded.

"Pure opium. Enough to cause death."

I placed my hand over my mouth and gasped. "Please do not tell me any more," I said gravely.

She met my glance with a look of regretful apology. "I know we are not friends, Miss Durnham. If you will forgive my previous behavior and listen to me . . . as a friend."

"The girl's life is at stake," I said, ignoring her overture. "That is all that matters."

"Exactly," she stated coolly. "I would like you and my daughter to leave your rooms in the tower, and reside in the little key house at the end of the courtyard. And I would like you to leave immediately. She is not safe for another minute."

Margaret regarded her daughter, who watched attentively with an air of childish wonder. She went to Victoria and kissed her cheek, then holding Victoria's chin in her cupped hand, surveyed her face, whispering an endearment that I could not hear. Patting Victoria's face distractedly, she came gliding back to me in a flutter of silk. And laid a key in my palm.

"Leave as soon as you can make yourself ready. Eva is on her way up with breakfast. Take it with you, if you can stow the rolls in your baggage."

"Yes."

"The house is located in the courtyard, opposite the keep and next to the Queen's Gate. You'll find it built into the inner curtain wall, next to the old weaver's cottage on the right and stables to the left. There's a lintel above the door, on which is carved the name 'Key House, 1610.'"

I said calmly, "Thank you, madam. And do not worry about your daughter. She will be safe with me until . . . better arrangements can be made."

She husked in an unsteady voice, "I know she will." Without looking back, she walked composedly past me and out the door.

The flight to the key house had been a rapid one. The morning mist still clung to the world and the cold stones crunched under our footfall. Clad in dark colors, we crept carefully across the inner courtyard until we found the little timber-framed house.

The narrow, low-ceiling abode was cheerful, with furniture out of the Tudor age. The slanting oak floor was buffed to a gloss, chairs were trimmed in gold curlicue, faded tapestries hung on the walls and covered the dining table, and at the windows hung rich draperies of gold-green. The room was filled with dozens of candles in wall sconces and two brass chandeliers above.

But for all the cottage's comforts, there could be no fire tonight, nor could we burn a lamp or light a candle. We could do nothing to betray our presence; even the curtains had to remain open, undisturbed. . . .

We made short shrift of unpacking. Victoria had brought along her easel and paints, yet her decision to do so made me uncomfortable. But it was diversion for her and could hardly be harmful, as long as no one saw her artwork. I brought along some books, but it was impossible to keep my mind on the material.

Fortunately Margaret had thought to supply us with dried meats, canned fruit, a wedge of hard cheese, and several bottles of expensive-looking wine. With our packet of fresh breakfast rolls, we would not go hungry for several days.

As dusk covered the land like a shadow I was able to go to the rippled windows, without fear of discovery, and peer out. There in the waning light of evening stood the keep. It floated on a cloud of newly gathering fog, two tiny lights blinking out at me, a fairy-tale castle, a Camelot. It was unbearable to think about the marquess up there in his tower—with Margaret.

By nine o'clock we were bunked down in the loft bed nestled in the steeple roof. The illusion of safety was comforting, but before we could indulge in sleep, someone knocked at the door.

My mind began to stampede in panic as a new fear washed over me. Who knew we were here? I clutched my heart, but didn't move.

I listened dazedly. Above the million tiny night noises—the creak of a settling board, a mouse in the wall, a branch of an oak tree against the timbers—I heard a voice calling. It was urgent, pleading me to let her in. And I was sure it was Margaret!

I climbed down the ladder and peeked out the window to see if it was, indeed, Margaret on the threshold. There she stood, her back to the wall of black sky, a cape over her shoulders, hood pulled up around her head, her face a pale blur.

I leaned against the door for a frozen second. My hand gripped the doorknob, but I held it there, immobile, riveted to the spot. There was a moment of uncertainty, but it washed over me quickly, like a wave of cold water, and left me trembling.

I had purposely disobeyed the marquess's instructions, and now I was putting all my trust with Margaret. Surely I had been right to do so. Yet what was so urgent that she had to come to our hiding place? This was dangerous. What if someone followed her?

She called to me through the barrier of door, taking hold of the latch and rattling it impatiently. I controlled my shaking hands. I cannot hesitate for another moment, I thought. This is no time to doubt my belief in Margaret, for the marquess was definitely setting a trap. To have followed him instead would have brought unequivocal disaster. Definitely. I opened the door.

She stood on the step, peering at me with her dark glistening eyes. Her skin, white as cotton, was drawn with tiny, pinched lines of worry.

She was talking in muted whispers. "He's gone to the lighthouse. He's searching for the jewels, I know he is. Oh, please come with me! Help me to catch him. He just left, and I saw him walk down there, across the lawns toward the—"

"The marquess?" I asked, and she began to cry.

I shuddered and turned away. "Of course," I mumbled to myself. Who else, indeed? But I could not let my despair play me false.

The Haunting of Victoria

She was crying softly into her handkerchief, and I faltered for a moment, glancing back at the loft. No movement from there.

"Would you like to step inside for a moment while I get my things?" I asked in a nervous little voice.

"Only . . . only for a moment. We must hurry. I'm sorry. It's so terrible . . . so terrible," she said in a suffocated whisper as she stepped inside the door.

"Yes, I know," I said numbly.

I ran for my cape and pulled it over my nightdress, knowing how ridiculous it must look. But there was no time. . . .

I fastened my shoes over cold, bare feet, and with my back carefully turned toward Margaret to conceal my actions, I pulled the sheathed knife out of the burlap bag that the marquess had given me. And stuck it in the waistband of my dress, under the cape.

My mind was whirling with too many fears to understand them all. This was the night Victoria and I were to leave the castle, according to the marquess's plans. Was he hiding out there on the lane, crouching in the brush, ready to spring? I had my doubts that he was digging for jewels tonight, as Margaret thought. But if he wasn't who were we following?

I turned toward the loft bed again, and suddenly Victoria sat bolt upright and stared down at us. It was impossible to see her shadowed face, but her rigid posture alerted me to her fear.

I glanced at Margaret, who tensely watched the girl. "It's going to be fine," I said aloud.

"Victoria . . ." Margaret sighed, her face pulled with distress.

I swooped up a pencil and paper, frantically warning Victoria that she must wait here for me to return, that as long as the door was locked, she would be safe. No one had the key but myself—I prayed this was true—but even so, under no circumstances, should she venture out from the loft until she was certain it was I who entered.

She nodded in bewildered acquiescence.

Margaret watched her child with helpless desperation. "She will not be harmed, if left alone?"

I hoped my wildly hammering heart did not divulge my uncertainty. "Of course not," I said with false confidence. "She will be fine, madam, until we return. I will lock the door behind us, and she will be safe."

Margaret placed a gloved hand on my arm. "Thank you," she said as she stepped out the door.

I threw one last, frenzied look at Victoria and blew her a kiss. Please, may she be safe, was all I could think as I followed Margaret into the silent darkness.

We glided along the stony path cautiously, slipping on the wet cobblestones, keeping close to the buildings, letting the cloak of night protect us. I was thankful that the darkness was deeper because of the fog.

We hurried through the Queen's Gate and across the lawns. Halfway along the rolling Downs, Margaret paused.

"Listen," she said.

We both listened. The gloom was filled with night sounds. A scurrying rodent scampered over the path, the impatient sea beat against shore, a twig snapped somewhere ahead of us.

"He's in there, hammering at the walls, looking for them. Can you hear it?"

I strained my ears, but heard no hammer. "I'm afraid I don't, madam."

"Then follow me. You will soon."

She stepped ahead purposefully, and I trod behind her, uneasy.

We came up to the looming pillar of lighthouse, and she stopped at the back of the building. She pulled her cloak tighter around her.

"I'm frightened," she rasped.

"Shall I lead the way now?" I offered. Then, as if to reassure myself as well as her: "We must not be nervous. There are two of us, and it will be easier to defend ourselves in the event . . . in case we may need to do so."

She quivered. "All right."

Slowly, muscles flexed for disaster, I led the way. We crept around to the stone-flagged entrance, and I fought to control my ragged breath. We both peered in. The room

The Haunting of Victoria

was eerily illuminated by a flickering torch on one wall—just above the place where I had noticed the fresh mortar yesterday. And where the mortar had been, there was a monstrous gaping hole that looked like a grotesque, giant mouth! But there was no priest.

We both jumped back, and I stifled a scream.

Margaret clamped her hand on my arm so tightly it hurt. "Move in," she whispered.

Summoning my wits, I slunk slowly toward the aperture in the wall, feeling Margaret close behind. I tried to get a glimpse down into the fathomless cavity. The torch wavered, and I saw a plank of old wood jutting out from the edge of a wooden frame. On the ledge sat a crudely carved metal box. This was the old well and an ancient receptacle for valuables! Catherine had been right all along. This was, undoubtedly, the hiding place for the infamous jewels. But the box was empty; the raider had taken the loot for himself.

Chill panic ripped through me. The marquess had trapped us. As surely as if he had led us here himself, as surely as he had done to Catherine!

"We must leave here at once," I heard myself uttering.

As I was turning back to Margaret I felt a rush of air at my back, saw her giant shadow lurch hideously upon the wall. I yanked myself away, just in time to escape being hurled down into the depths of the treacherous opening.

She laughed indulgently.

I wrenched around to face her and gasped.

She lowered her hood, the flash of brilliance around her neck catching the light. She pulled back her sleeves and displayed her wrists; the torchlight caught the burnished stones, a myriad of colors flashed across her skin. They were unmistakably the Rothesay jewels!

Chapter Thirteen

"YOU!" I SHRIEKED.

She smiled maniacally.

"You must admit I'm clever."

"But . . . but you have the jewels!"

"Yes, your sister helped me find them."

With labored breath, I held the wall for support. "My sister? How did you know? What have you done to her?"

"You are too inquisitive, don't you think?" She smiled coldly.

I felt the stiff wedge of knife still looped inside my skirt.

"But it wasn't difficult to figure out who you were, that you had come looking for your sister. She's down there, by the way." She gestured. "In the well. Where you are going to go meet her."

I was speechless with fear.

"You did give a nice performance, however. No one but me guessed that you really hadn't come to play teacher to Victoria."

"You knew who I . . . I was?"

She touched the scintillating stones at her neck. "Of course I knew. Your father was desperately worried over his daughter's disappearance and had to find Catherine. When he died suddenly, you came to replace him. Not out of duty or obligation, as you so humbly told James and me, but out of unquenched curiosity. It wasn't hard to figure. An American girl comes to Tavistock as an historian, she disappears, and six months later another American girl arrives.

There's a similarity between you and Catherine, by the way. I noticed it, and that . . . that ungrateful brat Victoria did, too."

"Ungrateful brat?" I repeated, stunned.

She watched me steadily, eyes glimmering with an unhealthy light. "She is not my child."

"No!" I cried, stunned, my thoughts confused. This was a nightmare, a terrible dream. I would wake shortly.

"Haven't you wondered who has been trying to kill her?"

"But that was the priest! The priest was creeping into her room at night . . . I saw him!"

She moved a little closer to the torch, trapping me closer to the edge of the hole. The light above her head flattened her features, making her look evil, more frightful.

Then I knew.

"It's . . . you are the priest!" I gasped in a strangled cry.

"How perceptive of you!" She laughed.

"But why? Why did you want to destroy the girl?"

She said in a deep, guttural tone: "I had no intention of destroying Victoria, at first. But she was too curious. My plan was so carefully laid. Everyone believed that I was Margaret Rothesay. I researched her background meticulously and even had forged papers to prove my identity. No one doubted that I was her. Even James. He thought I had survived the shipwreck in the South Pacific, and that I had returned to claim my daughter and my . . . fortune."

I faltered. What an ingenious plan!

"James, you see, was studying at the Sorbonne in Paris when the first Margaret met his mother and entrusted Victoria to her care. So no one in the present household knew the real Margaret."

"Except Victoria," I said.

"Only as an infant. Yet she sensed that something was wrong. She did not like me. She never warmed to me, and turned away from me at every corner. I was becoming very angry with her. You can imagine how difficult that made things," she said coldly.

"No wonder Victoria has been suffering so greatly!" I panted.

She frowned and inched toward me. I was trapped between the corner of the lighthouse and the yawning well opening.

"I would certainly not allow interference by a spoiled child like Victoria. I was here to find those famous jewels, and find them I would! I hadn't a clue where to look until your sister arrived. I knew she would lead me to them. I kept my eyes on her. And then on Halloween—"

"No!" I screamed.

"Yes." She took a step closer. "It was damp and foggy that night, like it is tonight. Miss Ryce was standing where you are now. Frightened, just like you. She had uncovered this wall—after almost three hundred years—and found that crude box balanced on the bucket ledge of the well. She was triumphant, the jewels spilling over in her hands."

"But she had not won—not yet. I had trapped her, and behind her was the black abyss of the well. She flung the jewels at me and begged to be set free. But don't you see that I couldn't do that? I had come too far. The jewels were mine, then!"

I flattened against the wall. "You are mad . . . mad!"

"No, not mad, ambitious," she said indignantly. "Just as I was pushing your poor, struggling sister down the well, Victoria happened upon us. The girl witnessed Catherine's screams as she plummeted down into the black tunnel that would become her grave. Victoria went pale with fright and opened her mouth to yell—but nothing came out. No sound. Before I could catch her, she flew back to the house and took to her bed, ill. I fretted and worried, what could I do with her? I knew she had to be gotten rid of. But then she awoke the next day with no voice, or hearing, or memory. And I was safe, until you arrived, and she began painting— those pictures. Victoria had to die before she revealed what I had done."

I flinched at her awful words.

"It was clever of me to lace her chocolate at night with mild doses of laudanum, wasn't it? To make her ill, then working up to stronger and stronger doses until she . . . would perish. It was made to look like part of her illness."

The Haunting of Victoria

She gleamed that sparkling smile of hers, so delighted with her craftiness, so eager for me to realize how skillful she had been.

I remembered Catherine's diary entries about how sick she had become on several occasions. "And you tried to poison Catherine, too!"

"Naturally."

"The portcullis gate in the dungeons," I wheezed. "Where I was trapped. That was you, wasn't it? Trying to kill me?"

She smiled maliciously.

"I knew the priest was after me—for encouraging Victoria to paint. I just never dreamed it was you!" I cried.

"That wasn't the only reason I wanted you and your blasted sister out of the way," she ground out.

I watched her face in the wavering glow of light, and tried to calculate how to move around her without getting caught.

"I wanted to get rid of both of you so I could win James's heart forever. Catherine thought she could gain his love, and she was dangerously close, mind you! And then you! You came along and tried to do the same, but you were both very wrong. You were competing against the wrong woman!"

"But the marquess is going to marry you!"

Suddenly she looked crestfallen. "He's never loved me, I always knew that. And when I got rid of Catherine, he went mad with grief. I had to make him mine forever, so I enticed him into my room one night."

She met my glance sharply. "Don't you see? I had to keep him!"

"Yes," I said, reaching slowly, slowly inside my cape, feeling for the band around my waist.

"He made love to me. Rough, lusty, taking me completely. And now I am with child." She gloated. "I told him the good news yesterday, and in order to keep his honor he changed the wedding date. Imagine! The week before that, he had tried to cancel the wedding altogether!"

I swallowed hard, my fingers touching the knobby knife case.

"I told him the best was yet to come. If he could wait until the wedding night, I had a great surprise for him. The jewels! Imagine how he will feel when I present these to him! He has waited for so long."

"Yes," I said, pulling the knife gently, gently from its sheath.

"You don't blame me for wanting James, do you?" and she came so close she practically touched me.

"No!" I sobbed, pulling out the steel blade.

It snagged on a thread, and I fumbled with it a moment before she realized what I was doing. Then she was upon me, trying to yank the dangerous weapon from my hands.

"Help me! Help me!" I cried, hysteria threatening to overtake me.

She ripped the blade from me, tearing a gash in my hand. Warm liquid poured down my arm, but I was unaware of it until I saw the smear of blood on her bodice. My shoulders ached and my hand was on fire as I tried to wrestle free of her mighty grip.

Finally, with a herculean attempt, I broke free of her fierce strength and hurled myself toward the door. I heard her grunt with effort as she heaved herself after me. I lunged to one side to escape her attack, but was too late. The full force of her body crashed into me, a projectile of human strength hurtling me onto my back.

I lay sprawled on the ground, stunned and gasping for breath. At last my flattened lungs filled with air, and I swallowed in quick, choking inhalations, waiting for the knife to dig into my skin.

Then I heard a scream. It was not my own voice, but a younger, higher, childish voice. My head spun and darkness closed in.

I thought I was dreaming, haunted by images of the marquess. He squeezed my hand tightly, and its warmth was soothing. I felt him lean close to me; his face grazed my cheek and he whispered like a sigh, "Please wake up."

I started out of my unconsciousness, and my eyes stared into Rothesay's deep, fathomless ones. I was not dreaming. This was real!

"Are you all right? Your hand is . . . does it hurt badly?" His voice was soft as satin.

A sharp stab of pain in my right hand reminded me of the grisly scene in the lighthouse. I lifted my arm slightly and saw that my hand had been carefully wrapped in gauze.

"I'm fine, though I've never had such a shock." I wanted to sit up, but remembering that I had fainted, I did not struggle.

I looked around the room dazedly. I was resting on my sofa by the hearth in my own deeply shadowed room. I turned to the dancing flames. Hot tongues licked out from under the dry logs, warming me delightfully.

"How long have I been here?" It was a weak question, but I felt compelled to say something. The marquess watched me darkly, unmoving, before answering.

"It is nearly two in the morning. You have slept for several hours. Though it seems an eternity." He exhaled through clenched teeth.

He tightened his clasp on my left hand, and I thought how incongruous it was that its warmth comforted me, when only hours before . . .

There had to be endless explanations, but for now it only mattered that he was here with me, holding my hand.

"So it was her all the time," I said quietly.

There was silence.

I looked at him, saw the shadow of beard on his finely carved jaw, the twitch of muscle as he stared away from me into the snapping fire.

"Yes," he said hoarsely. But he offered nothing more.

"The doctor has been in to see you." He pulled his hand away and reached into his rumpled jacket. "Do you mind?" He removed a pipe.

"No, of course not."

He held a long taper to his pipe and inhaled long and deeply for a moment. "The doctor said you would be fine, that you seemed to have survived the shock all right. But you looked so white and frail"—his voice was thick with emotion—"that I wondered if you . . . were going to—"

There was a high, sweet giggle from behind him. "We both worried about you, Miss Durnham! We were so frightened for you! I prayed that you would live."

Victoria bounded into view from behind the painted screen that stood protectively against one side of my bed. Her face beamed with happiness. Now I knew why the marquess could not venture to say more about Margaret.

"Victoria!" I caught my breath and tried to keep the burning tears of joy in check.

She sidled past her uncle—smiling up at him as he nodded gently to her—and sat on the edge of my bed. "I can talk to you now, and hear you, too. I'm better now. I'm cured, and it's all because of you." Her voice was clear as a nightingale's song.

I laughed. "You're giving me a lot of credit for something that I had no part in!"

Unable to contain her thrill at being unburdened of her terrible affliction, she jumped up and twirled about. She was no longer a prisoner of that grim cave, as in the marquess's story. She was set free, and now her dark days were over.

"Isn't it lovely?"

The unchecked tears were foolishly rolling down my face. I told her that hearing her speak was the sweetest melody I had ever heard.

At the marquess's insistence, she sat down again, but I could see that she could barely contain her exuberance.

"You've had a miraculous escape," the marquess said softly to me. "Are you hungry? I have made some sandwiches and tea."

"I'm famished," Victoria chimed in.

Remembering that our last meal had been way before sunset, I agreed that a sandwich and tea would be grand.

The marquess produced a tray with delicate little sandwiches filled with a sort of cheese with cucumber and sliced cold beef. I drank the warm tea, the strong liquid reviving me almost immediately. Victoria and I ate and exclaimed together while the marquess sank into a chair by the fire and watched us with the pleasure of a benevolent uncle.

As I swallowed the last bite of a sandwich and sipped the strong, dark tea, I met the marquess's steady gaze. "Well . . . ? How long must you keep me in suspense?" A bitter smile twisted my lips. "I think it's time one of you gave me an account of what happened."

Victoria shot a pensive look at her uncle. "Please, may I tell her? I've been waiting . . ."

There was a glint of light in his frown. He looked at me, then back to his niece.

"All right, Victoria. Tell her what she has to be told, and then you must go to bed."

Victoria nestled down next to me and began to talk. We sat there like that, I propped against my lacy pillows, Victoria on my bed, eagerly going over the whole affair, reviewing our harrowing experiences for a long while. The marquess smoked and occasionally interjected what he knew. It is impossible to recall everything that was said, but when the dark clouds of night swept out over the ocean and dawn glowed around the shutters, I knew that this was an important turning point in my life.

The story was pretty much as I had thought. Victoria completed her third painting yesterday—during our stay in the key house. It had revealed the face of the priest. It was, of course, Margaret.

Victoria was terribly frightened by this and decided not to show me. She still had not recovered her faculties and did not understand why her head had guided her hand to paint such a horrible picture.

"Some inner voice prompted me to complete my painting by the end of the day," she told me. "So when my mother came to get you at the cottage, I was afraid. I could not believe that she was a murderess, but I realized she was not your friend, as she pretended to be. I . . . I just couldn't understand what was happening. Something was not right, and I didn't know what it was. I only knew I had to follow you."

"It was you I heard scream, then?"

"Yes. When I saw her lunge at you, it brought reeling back that terrible image of when she pushed Miss Ryce down that... that hole in the wall."

"And that shock must have revived your senses?" I asked with wonderment in my voice.

"Yes, yes... I was so scared. So horrified to see my mother... and I gasped and stood paralyzed. But this time a loud, piercing scream came from my throat. That's when she saw me, and left you lying on the ground and came forward... toward me and..." Her voice cracked and tears spilled down her cheeks.

Her uncle was at her side in seconds, tenderly handing her a handkerchief. "I told you it would only pain you to tell her. You are brave, Victoria. But I don't want to see you become ill again. You have been so weakened by all this stress."

She shot him a quick, scornful look. "I will never be ill again, Uncle! Don't you see that I am cured. I know the truth now, and that is all I have ever wanted."

"So it is," he said grimly.

She flung herself next to me. "Miss Durnham, I was so afraid... so afraid of my mother that I couldn't move. And then Hal Mathews came running up out of nowhere and dragged her away from me. She was screaming and kicking and flaying her arms wildly... and I kept saying, 'Mother! Mother!' and do you know what she said?"

Her tone was uneven, faltering, and though her eyes glistened, they were steady; the tears did not fall.

"I don't know," I said quietly.

"She said that I wasn't her child! That she was a fake, and I was a foolish girl!"

I cringed. So she did know! I glanced at the marquess. He stood behind Victoria, watching her with concern.

"I knew then that I was right all along. I distrusted her from the moment she arrived here and said she was my mother. But everyone loved her so, and I thought... well, I am a child and could not say that I didn't like her. So I pretended to love her, too. After all, a child must respect adults!"

"How horrible for you," I uttered sadly.

"Once my voice had returned, I figured out it was she who had poisoned me, she who wanted me dead! I hope she dies now! I think we should hang her on the rack in the oubliettes and watch her suffer! How she deserves to be tortured for what she did . . . to you, to Miss Ryce . . . to me!" Her voice was pitched toward hysteria.

The marquess heaved a long shivering sigh and touched Victoria lightly on her elbow. She rose and stood limply by my bed. He strode to the door and pulled the braided bell pull to summon Eva.

Before Victoria was ushered from my room, she bent to me and kissed my cheek. "Good-bye for now, Miss Anne. You will always be my friend! Always."

Eva pulled the door closed with a soft click, leaving me alone to face the marquess—and my future.

He went immediately to the windows to open the shutters. The morning light poured in. He moved to the fireplace, crossing his arms over the mantel and resting his chin there. How badly I wanted to go to him and bring his attention back to me, but he seemed stern and distant.

"What will become of us?" he asked gravely.

I looked down at my fluffy counterpane but could not answer.

"We hide behind our masks, but we fool no one," he continued drearily. "Even if we build a house of stone to protect ourselves, there is no sure refuge. At every front door there is a worn step, an unlevel patch to throw one."

He turned to me, his winged brows drawn into a scowl.

"As I have hidden behind my own mask," I admitted.

"As we all have," he said flatly.

My gaze shifted, and I looked away.

He wiped a hand across his face and sank into a chair facing my bed. His stiff collar was unbuttoned and jutted out from his neck, his shirt was rumpled, his jacket hung loosely on his lean frame. A shadow passed over his face, and in that instant I was sorrier for him than for his niece.

"Margaret's real name is Sarah. My mother was in love with her father once—Hal Mathews, the gatehouse keeper."

"Margaret's father is the gatehouse keeper?" I asked incredulously.

"Yes." He nodded unhappily.

I exhaled a chill breath. The horrible pieces of puzzle were beginning to fit! Hal had warned me that someone didn't like what I was doing, and according to Victoria, he had saved the girl's life when Margaret tried to kill her. He must have known what his daughter was capable of!

"His real name is Richard Rashleigh, and he is from the impoverished Rashleigh family in Dover. When he hired on here as a stable master many years ago, my mother could not resist him. He was a real lady-killer in his day—swarthy, handsome, dapper. She tried to elope with him, but they were found and brought back to Tavistock. He was sent away, but he returned, for he wanted more than my mother's love, he wanted her money. He broke into my grandfather's keep one night and was caught stealing the family silver plate. He was deported at once to Australia."

"His unusual accent," I breathed to myself.

He cocked his head, appraising me. "Yes," he said before continuing.

"Eventually my mother was married to my father. I doubt that Mother was ever happy." He looked away for a moment, his brow furrowed.

"My father was twenty years her senior, but it was a suitable social match. From their union was born my elder brother, Ninian, and myself. When Ninian became a young man, he met a woman named Margaret." He returned his look to me. "You know this story. They fell in love, married, and sailed to the South Pacific shortly after their daughter, Victoria, was born. To be lost forever."

I nodded.

"I never met Margaret, so when Mother passed away and I took custody of Victoria, I had never laid eyes on the baby's mother." He paused and smiled gravely.

"Meanwhile Hal had a daughter of his own, a grown-up daughter, and he envisioned that she would marry for money—as he had not. When his wife died, he formulated a plan. He knew a lot about our family—especially about

The Haunting of Victoria

the heirloom jewels hidden in the castle—and decided to apply for a position as gatehouse keeper. There were actual rumors of a ghost priest walking the grounds, you know. All the better. He could use the costume to masquerade as a ghost at night while searching for the stones. No one could discover his identity that way."

"But I thought Margaret was the priest?"

"She was, also. They were working together, you see. Let me backtrack a moment. Richard, *née* Hal, arrived at Tavistock six months before his daughter. They had researched well, and knew that I had never met Margaret."

"And when Margaret, or Sarah, arrived, they began working together to find the jewels?" I asked.

"Yes. It was set up that Richard would wear the robe at night and pose as a ghost. Sarah planned to flirt outrageously with me and keep me sidetracked long enough for Richard to do some serious searching for jewels. But their great plot ran afoul when Sarah fell in love with me."

I lowered my head.

"And when she sensed that I was falling in love with Catherine Ryce, the plans really began to backfire."

I met his look once more.

"I'm sorry," he said quietly.

"And when Catherine found the jewels?" I asked.

"Richard knew nothing of that. It seems that Margaret took the robe on her own and posed as the priest. She was losing enthusiasm for working with her father. Unfortunately, at that point, I counted more to her than the jewels, but she knew how much I wanted the gems. Her revised plan was to get to the jewels before her father and give them to me. She had no intention of including her father in this scheme. I have no idea how much Richard suspected her, but he must have guessed that she had something to do with Catherine's disappearance since he showed up last night to save Victoria."

He stretched his long legs before him, and brushed his hands over the arms of the chair. "And once Catherine was gone, Richard must have guessed that Sarah was trying to murder Victoria, for who else would want the girl out of the way? But I don't think he knew that Sarah actually had the jewels, because he was still searching for them," the marquess continued.

I thought of my dreadful confrontation with the gate-house keeper in the lighthouse the day before. "So even yesterday when he warned me that I was in danger, he was searching?"

The marquess nodded.

"Why did he care that my life might be endangered?"

"He didn't want any more missing people until he had secured the jewels. Then he could leave, or take Sarah, whatever," the marquess answered grimly.

"But he knew that Sarah wasn't coming with him. If he left, that is. He knew that she was in love with you."

Another silence.

Then he said in a strained voice, "Sarah knew how to play the role of a rich widow, how to inspire my compassion. And passion. She was so beautiful . . ."

He lowered his head and covered his face. I watched him, and when he looked up again, his eyes bored into mine.

"Can you forgive me a little, Anne?"

"It is I who must be forgiven," I said, but my miserable words sounded forced and unnatural.

He leaned forward, looking squarely at me. "For what, Anne?"

"For not trusting you. For running right into Margar— Sarah's trap. And all along I knew . . ." And then I asked the question that I never intended to ask.

"Did you love her a little?"

He said, very seriously, "I stayed with her not because I loved her, but because I suspected that she might not be who she said she was. I wanted to trap her, to make her pay for her evil deeds. Little did I dream how much I was to pay as well!" he hissed.

His eyes were cold, distant, and he didn't meet my gaze. I wanted to bring him back to things as they were now, to tell him that we could build anew over the ruins, but I couldn't. Not yet. Instead I threw my robe over my shoulders and

The Haunting of Victoria

went to him and knelt at his feet. I laid my head in his lap, and he stroked my hair gently, tenderly. Neither of us spoke for a long time.

I heard the ravishing songs of birds outside my window, the clock chimed eight o'clock. How deceptively quiet and untouched by tragedy my little room was.

When he spoke again, his voice was hoarse and deep. "Did you really think I killed your sister?"

"No, never. I don't think I ever did believe that."

A strained pause. "I think you understand me."

"Yes, I do," I said thickly, raising my head. "And even when I was running away from you, trying to save Victoria's life, even as the world was careening madly out of control, I must have known, must have felt deep down, that I understood you, and that you weren't really guilty."

A door slammed in the distance, and I heard footsteps racing along the corridors, getting heavier as they approached. There was a sharp banging on my door. I stood up and let the marquess answer the summons.

It was unmistakably Hal's voice. Though I could not see him, it was pitifully obvious that he was crying. His voice broke between a wail and a plead, and my heart leaped for him.

"She's gone . . . she's gone, sir. My beautiful daughter! She drank it all. The rest of the laudanum. It was empty when I found her, there was enough in that bottle to . . . oh, God! How could she do it? How can I live without her . . . ?" His voice trailed off into a muffled sob.

The marquess shot me a sideways glance and disappeared behind the door.

I was crying again, too. Crying for Margaret, for my sister, for Victoria. How I wished this could have ended neatly, and without pain. That I could have found Catherine alive, and we would all live happily ever after.

But this was not a fairy-tale castle, and Catherine was not here any longer. Whether I wanted to admit it or not, life for me was changed forever. There was a great chasm between the old life and the new, and I knew it had to be crossed once and for all.

As if knowing these changes in my life would be easier to bear by keeping busy, I bathed, dressed in a spring teal traveling suit, and contacted Gavin about the next train departure from town. He would take me to the depot as soon as I was ready.

I was packing when the marquess knocked at my door again later that morning. I opened it, and he drew me into his arms without speaking. He was gentle when he kissed me. It was forgiving and tender, and I melted in his assured embrace, hearing his heart pound through the thin silk of my dress.

When he released me, he looked around my room. "Where are you going?"

"Gavin will take me to town to catch the train into London. I—I didn't think that staying here was a good idea."

His hands clenched. "Didn't you think about Victoria? About how much she would need you."

My heart was hurting. "She needs a mother, not an art teacher. I've taught her all I know, but she is a young woman now and has other needs."

"Needs that an uncle cannot understand." Under his quiet voice was that tone that I recognized. "Anne?"

He was standing very close now, and I heard him catch his breath.

"Yes?"

He reached for my injured hand as if he touched china. Cradling it delicately between his muscular ones, he said, "I have never been married before, and I am not sure how to go about this sort of thing, to be honest."

I trembled, but didn't answer.

He smiled, but his eyes were dark. Those snapping, liquid eyes that knew everything. "Now that Richard is on his way to Australia again, and his daughter has met her death by her own hands, I suppose you think it would be best to finish packing and hurry back to your life in New York?"

"Yes, I felt it would be a wise thing to do." My voice quavered.

"Well, you are not going to."

The Haunting of Victoria

He laughed suddenly, a rich, baritone chuckle, his face creasing with dimples. He pulled me to him again, but this time he was not gentle. His kiss was insatiable, relentless, his arms were steel around my neck. Abruptly he pulled away and held my shoulders firmly.

"You are going to stay here with me, whether it is wise or not, because I love you. And someday soon you will wear those sparkling diamonds 'round your neck as befits a new Rothesay bride. And people will mock you and think you married me for my money, and that you were a fool to do so."

"But . . . but are you asking me to marry you?" I asked foolishly, humbly.

His face became serious. He stared into my eyes somberly.

"Yes. Are you prepared?"

I faltered. "Prepared?"

"It will be difficult married to a man like me."

"Of course, a man in your position . . ."

"That's just it. It's a damnable position, full of responsibility and sacrifice."

"I'm used to that."

"Townspeople will whisper behind your back. It may take months, years, to be fully accepted here."

"But I'll have you by my side."

"Not always. I travel a lot. Many times for a month or two at a time. Sometimes I will take you with me, but they will be seldom."

I smiled through the nervousness I felt. "This is a strange marriage proposal. You seem determined to talk me out of saying yes."

"Not at all. I won't let you say no. It's just that I want you to know the truth, since there has been . . . so little of it around here lately."

I knew this was no time for polite banter, so I bit my lip and plunged ahead.

"Very well, let's speak honestly. Are you saying that you can be happily married to a woman like me . . . a woman who knows nothing of society?" I asked boldly.

He smiled again. His teeth sparkled, his eyes were warm. "From the moment I saw you, I knew. But I could not tell you what I felt, could not approach you. You believed that I loved someone else, and what could I say to make you think otherwise?"

He lowered his gaze. "I spent many burning nights with you on my mind. But you could not know, I could not divulge my secret. Until now."

Liquid fire seared through my veins. "Nor could I say what I felt," I whispered.

He watched me under his heavy brows. "What do you say, Anne? You have not answered my question."

"Yes, I will be your wife, if you're willing to take a chance on a plain girl from New York who likes to paint pictures."

He laughed, and it sounded amazingly relieved. "Never underestimate how blazingly important you are to me."

I laughed, too, then, and slanted a look up at him. "And will I have been a fool to marry you, like they will all say?"

He did not answer, but pulled me to him again, and I could not see his expression. But it didn't matter. Because I already knew.

And after a few minutes I began to unpack.